NEVER BETRAY A DORSAI!

He was obviously about to betray our presence, and Amanda did exactly the correct thing . . . She uncoiled from the ground like a spring released from tension, one fist taking the fugitive in the Adam's apple to cut off his cry and the other going into him just under the breastbone to take the wind out of him and put him down without killing him.

As she took the man down, another shot sounded from the pursuers, clearly aimed at the now stationary target of the fugitive—and Amanda went down with him. . . .

Tor books by Gordon R. Dickson

Alien Art
Arcturus Landing
Beyond the Dar Al-Harb
Dorsai
The Dragon Knight
The Far Call
The Final Encyclopedia
Gremlins Go Home (with Ben Bova)
Guided Tour
Hoka! (with Poul Anderson)
Home from the Shore
The Last Master
Love Not Human
The Man From Earth
The Man the Worlds Rejected
Mission to Universe
On the Run
The Outposter
The Pritcher Mass
Pro
Sleepwalkers' World
Soldier, Ask Not
The Space Swimmers
Space Winners
Spacepaw
Spacial Delivery
The Spirit of Dorsai
Steel Brother
The Stranger
Wolf and Iron
Young Bleys

LOST DORSAI

THE NEW DORSAI COMPANION

GORDON R. DICKSON

A TOM DOHERTY ASSOCIATES BOOK
NEW YORK

This is a work of fiction. All the characters and events portrayed in this book are fictitious, and any resemblance to real people or events is purely coincidental.

LOST DORSAI © 1980 by Gordon R. Dickson
WARRIOR © 1965 by Gordon R. Dickson
A CHILDE CYCLE CONCORDANCE © 1993 by David W. Wixon

Cover art by Royo

A Tor Book
Published by Tom Doherty Associates, Inc.
175 Fifth Avenue
New York, N.Y. 10010

Tor ® is a registered trademark of Tom Doherty Associates, Inc.

ISBN: 0-812-50404-6

First edition: June 1993

Printed in the United States of America

0 9 8 7 6 5 4 3 2 1

CONTENTS

LOST DORSAI

I am Corunna El Man.

I brought the little courier vessel down at last at the spaceport of Nahar City on Ceta, the large world around Tau Ceti. I had made it from the Dorsai in six phase shifts to transport, to the stronghold of Gebel Nahar, our Amanda Morgan—she whom they call the Second Amanda.

Normally I am far too senior in rank to act as a courier pilot. But I had been home on leave at the time. The courier vessels owned by the Dorsai Cantons are too expensive to risk lightly, but the situation required a contracts expert at Nahar more swiftly than one could safety be gotten there. They had asked me to take on the problem, and I had solved it by stretching the possibilities on each of the phase shifts, coming here.

The risks I had taken had not seemed to bother Amanda. That was not surprising, since she was Dorsai. But neither did she talk to me much on the trip; and that was a thing that had come to be, with me, a little unusual.

For things had been different for me after Baunpore. In the massacre there following the siege, when the North Freilanders finally overran the town, they cut up my face for the revenge of it; and they killed Else, for no other reason than that she was my wife. There was nothing left of her then but incandescent gas, dissipating throughout the universe; and since there could be no hope of a grave, nothing to come back to, nor any place where she could be remembered, I rejected surgery then, and chose to wear my scars as a memorial to her.

It was a decision I never regretted. But it was true that with those scars came an alteration in the way other people reacted to me. With some I found that I became almost invisible; and nearly all seemed to relax their natural impulse to keep private their personal secrets and concerns.

It was almost as if they felt that somehow I was now beyond the point where I would stand in judgment on their pains and sorrows. No, on second thought, it was something even stronger than that. It was as if I was like a burnt-out candle in the dark room of their inner selves—a lightless, but safe, companion whose presence reassured them that their privacy was still unbreached. I doubt very much that Amanda and those I was to meet on this trip to Gebel Nahar would have talked to me as freely as they later did, if I had met them back in the days when I had had Else, alive.

We were lucky on our incoming. The Gebel Nahar is more a mountain fortress than a palace or government center; and for military reasons Nahar City, near it, has a spaceport capable of handling deep-space ships. We debarked, expecting to be met in the terminal the minute we entered it through its field doors. But we were not.

The principality of Nahar Colony lies in tropical latitudes on Ceta, and the main lobby of the terminal was small, but high-ceilinged and airy; its floor and ceiling tiled in bright colors, with plants growing in planter areas all about; and bright, enormous, heavily-framed paintings on all the walls. We stood in the middle of all this and foot traffic moved past and around us. No one looked directly at us, although neither I with my scars, nor Amanda—who bore a remarkable resemblance to those pictures of the first Amanda in our Dorsai history books—were easy to ignore.

I went over to check with the message desk and found nothing there for us. Coming back, I had to hunt for Amanda, who had stepped away from where I had left her.

"El Man—" her voice said without warning, behind me. "Look!"

Her tone had warned me, even as I turned. I caught sight of her and the painting she was looking at, all in the same moment. It was high up on one of the walls; and she stood just below it, gazing up.

Sunlight through the transparent front wall of the terminal flooded her and the picture, alike. She was in all the natural colors of life—as Else had been—tall, slim, in light blue cloth jacket and short cream-colored skirt, with white-blond hair and that incredible youthfulness that her namesake ancestor had also owned. In contrast, the painting was rich in garish pigments, gold leaf and alizarin crimson, the human figures it depicted caught in exaggerated, melodramatic attitudes.

Leto de muerte, the large brass plate below it read. *Hero's Death-Couch*, as the title would roughly translate from the bastard, archaic Spanish spoken by the Naharese. It showed a great, golden bed set out on an open plain in the aftermath of the battle. All about were corpses and bandaged officers standing in gilt-encrusted uniforms. The living surrounded the bed

and its occupant, the dead Hero, who, powerfully muscled yet emaciated, hideously wounded and
stripped to the waist, lay upon a thick pile of velvet
cloaks, jewelled weapons, marvellously-wrought tap-
estries and golden utensils, all of which covered the
bed.

The body lay on its back, chin pointing at the sky,
face gaunt with the agony of death, still firmly holding by one large hand to its naked chest, the hilt of
an oversized and ornate sword, its massive blade
darkened with blood. The wounded officers standing
about and gazing at the corpse were posed in dramatic attitudes. In the foreground, on the earth beside
the bed, a single ordinary soldier in battle-torn uniform, dying, stretched forth one arm in tribute to the
dead man.

Amanda looked at me for a second as I moved
up beside her. She did not say anything. It was not
necessary to say anything. In order to live, for
two hundred years we on the Dorsai have exported
the only commodity we owned—the lives of our
generations—to be spent in wars for others' causes.
We live with real war; and to those who do that, a
painting like this one was close to obscenity.

"So that's how they think here," said Amanda.

I looked sideways and down at her. Along with
the appearance of her ancestor, she had inherited
the First Amanda's incredible youthfulness. Even I,
who knew she was only a half-dozen years younger
than myself—and I was now in my mid-thirties—
occasionally forgot that fact, and was jolted by the

realization that she thought like my generation rather than like the stripling she seemed to be.

"Every culture has its own fantasies," I said. "And this culture's Hispanic, at least in heritage."

"Less than ten percent of the Naharese population's Hispanic nowadays, I understand," she answered. "Besides, this is a caricature of Hispanic attitudes."

She was right. Nahar had originally been colonized by immigrants—Gallegos from the northwest of Spain who had dreamed of large ranches in a large open Territory. Instead, Nahar, squeezed by its more industrial and affluent neighbors, had become a crowded, small country which had retained a bastard version of the Spanish language as its native tongue and a medley of half-remembered Spanish attitudes and customs as its culture. After the first wave of immigrants, those who came to settle here were of anything but Hispanic ancestry, but still they had adopted the language and ways they found here.

The original ranchers had become enormously rich—for though Ceta was a sparsely populated planet, it was food-poor. The later arrivals swelled the cities of Nahar, and stayed poor—very poor.

"I hope the people I'm to talk to are going to have more than ten per cent of ordinary sense," Amanda said. "This picture makes me wonder if they don't prefer fantasy. If that's the way it is at Gebel Nahar . . ."

She left the sentence unfinished, shook her head, and then—apparently pushing the picture from her mind—smiled at me. The smile lit up her face, in

7 ■

something more then the usual sense of that phrase.
With her, it was something different, an inward light-
ing deeper and greater than those words usually indi-
cate. I had only met her for the first time, three days
earlier, and Else was all I had ever or would ever
want; but now I could see what people had meant on
the Dorsai, when they had said she inherited the first
Amanda's abilities to both command others and
make them love her.

"No message for us?" she said.

"No—" I began. But then I turned, for out of the
corner of my eye I had seen someone approaching
us.

She also turned. Our attention had been caught because the man striding toward us on long legs was a
Dorsai. He was big. Not the size of the Graeme
twins, Ian and Kensie, who were in command at
Gebel Nahar on the Naharese contract; but close to
that size and noticeably larger than I was. However,
Dorsai come in all shapes and sizes. What had identified him to us—and obviously, us to him—was not
his size but a multitude of small signals, too subtle to
be catalogued. He wore a Naharese army bandmaster's uniform, with warrant officer tabs at the collar;
and he was blond-haired, lean-faced, and no more
than in his early twenties. I recognized him.

He was a third son of a neighbor from my own
canton of High Island, on the Dorsai. His name was
Michael de Sandoval, and little had been heard of
him for six years.

"Sir—Ma'm," he said, stopping in front of us.

"Sorry to keep you waiting. There was a problem getting transport."

"Michael," I said. "Have you met Amanda Morgan?"

"No, I haven't." He turned to her. "An honor to meet you, ma'm. I suppose you're tired of having everyone say they recognize you from your great-grandmother's pictures?"

"Never tire of it," said Amanda cheerfully; and gave him her hand. "But you already know Corunna El Man?"

"The El Man family are High Island neighbors," said Michael. He smiled for a second, almost sadly, at me. "I remember the Captain from when I was only six years old and he was first home on leave. If you'll come along with me, please? I've already got your luggage in the bus."

"Bus?" I said, as we followed him toward one of the window-wall exits from the terminal.

"The band bus for Third Regiment. It was all I could get."

We emerged on to a small parking pad scattered with a number of atmosphere flyers and ground vehicles. Michael de Sandoval led us to a stubby-framed, powered lifting body, that looked as if it could hold about thirty passengers. Inside, one person saved the vehicle from being completely empty. It was an Exotic in a dark blue robe, an Exotic with white hair and a strangely ageless face. He could have been anywhere between thirty and eighty years of age and he was seated in the lounge area at the front of the bus, just before the compartment wall that divided off the control area in the vehicle's nose. He stood up as we came in.

"Padma, Outbond to Ceta," said Michael. "Sir, may I introduce Amanda Morgan, Contracts Adjuster, and Corunna El Man, Senior Ship Captain, both from the Dorsai? Captain El Man just brought the Adjuster in by courier."

"Of course, I know about their coming," said Padma.

He did not offer a hand to either of us. But, like many of the advanced Exotics I have known, he did not seem to need to. As with those others, there was a warmth and peace about him that the rest of us were immediately caught up in, and any behavior on his part seemed natural and expected.

We sat down together. Michael ducked into the control compartment, and a moment later, with a soft vibration, the bus lifted from the parking pad.

"It's an honor to meet you, Outbond," said Amanda. "But it's even more of an honor to have you meet us. What rates us that sort of attention?"

Padma smiled slightly.

"I'm afraid I didn't come just to meet you," he said to her. "Although Kensie Graeme's been telling me all about you; and—" he looked over at me, "even I've heard of Corunna El Man."

"Is there anything you Exotics don't hear about?" I said.

"Many things," he shook his head, gently but seriously.

"What was the other reason that brought you to the spaceport, then?" Amanda asked.

He looked at her thoughtfully.

"Something that has nothing to do with your coming," he said. "It happens I had a call to make to elsewhere on the planet, and the phones at Gebel Nahar are not as private as I liked. When I heard Michael was coming to get you, I rode along to make my call from the terminal, here."

"It wasn't a call on behalf of the Conde of Nahar, then?" I asked.

"If it was—or if it was for anyone but myself—" he smiled. "I wouldn't want to betray a confidence by admitting it. I take it you know about El Conde? The titular ruler of Nahar?"

"I've been briefing myself on the Colony and on Gebel Nahar ever since it turned out I needed to come here," Amanda answered.

I could see her signalling me to leave her alone with him. It showed in the way she sat and the angle at which she held her head. Exotics were perceptive, but I doubted that Padma had picked up that subtle private message.

"Excuse me," I told them. "I think I'll go have a word with Michael."

I got up and went through the door into the control section, closing it behind me. Michael sat relaxed, one hand on the control rod; and I sat down myself in the copilot's seat.

"How are things at home, sir?" he asked, without turning his head from the sky ahead of us.

"I've only been back this once since you'd have

left, yourself," I said. "But it hasn't changed much. My father died last year."

"I'm sorry to hear that."

"Your father and mother are well—and I hear your brothers are all right, out among the stars," I said. "But, of course, you know that."

"No," he said, still watching the sky ahead. "I haven't heard for quite a while."

A silence threatened.

"How did you happen to end up here?" I asked. It was almost a ritual question between Dorsais away from home.

"I heard about Nahar. I thought I'd take a look at it."

"Did you know it was as fake Hispanic as it is?"

"Not fake," he said. "Something . . . but not that." He was right, of course.

"Yes," I said, "I guess I shouldn't use the word fake. Situations like the one here come out of natural causes, like all others."

He looked directly at me. I had learned to read such looks since Else died. He was very close in that moment to telling me something more than he would probably have told anyone else. But the moment passed and he looked back out the windshield.

"You know the situation here?" he said.

"No. That's Amanda's job," I said. "I'm just a driver on this trip. Why don't you fill me in?"

"You must know some of it already," he said, "and Ian or Kensie Graeme will be telling you the rest. But in any case . . . the Conde's a figurehead. Literally. His father was set up with that title by the first

Naharese immigrants, who're all now rich ranchers. They had a dream of starting their own hereditary aristocracy here, but that never really worked. Still, on paper, the Conde's the hereditary sovereign of Nahar; and, in theory, the army belongs to him as Commander-in-Chief. But the army's always been drawn from the poor of Nahar—the city poor and the *campesinos*; and they hate the rich first-immigrants. Now there's a revolution brewing and the army doesn't know which way it'll jump."

"I see," I said. "So a violent change of government is on the way, and our contract here's with a government which may be out of power tomorrow. Amanda's got a problem."

"It's everyone's problem," Michael said. "The only reason the army hasn't declared itself for the revolutionaries is because its parts don't work together too well. Coming from the outside, the way you have, the ridiculousness of the locals' attitudes may be what catches your notice first. But actually those attitudes are all the non-rich have, here, outside of a bare existence—this business of the flags, the uniforms, the music, the duels over one wrong glance and the idea of dying for your regiment—or being ready to go at the throat of any other regiment at the drop of a hat."

"But," I said, "what you're describing isn't any practical, working sort of military force."

"No. That's why Kensie and Ian were contracted in here, to do something about turning the local army into something like an actual defensive force. The other principalities around Nahar all have their eyes on the ranchlands, here. Given a normal situation, the Graemes'd already be making progress—you know Ian's reputation for training troops. But the way it's turned out, the common soldiers here think of the Graemes as tools of the ranchers, the revolutionaries preach that they ought to be thrown out, and the regiments are non-cooperating with them. I don't think they've got a hope of doing anything useful with the army under present conditions; and the situation's been getting more dangerous daily—for them, and now for you and Amanda, as well. The truth is, I think Kensie and Ian'd be wise to take their loss on the contract and get out."

"If accepting loss and leaving was all there was to it, someone like Amanda wouldn't be needed here," I said. "There has to be more than that to involve the Dorsai in general."

He said nothing.

"How about you?" I said. "What's your position here? You're Dorsai too."

"Am I?" he said to the windshield, in a low voice.

I had at last touched on what had been going unspoken between us. There was a name for individuals like Michael, back home. They were called "lost Dorsai." The name was not used for those who had chosen to do something other than a military vocation. It was reserved for those of Dorsai heritage who seemed to have chosen their life work, whatever it was, and then—suddenly and without explanation—abandoned it. In Michael's case, as I knew, he had graduated from the Academy with honors; but after graduation he had abruptly withdrawn his name from assignment and left the planet, with no explanation, even to his family.

"I'm Bandmaster of the Third Naharese Regiment," he said, now. "My regiment likes me. The local people don't class me with the rest of you, generally—" he smiled a little sadly, again, "except that I don't get challenged to duels."

"I see," I said.

"Yes." He looked over at me now. "So, while the army is still technically obedient to the Conde, as its Commander-in-Chief, actually just about everything's come to a halt. That's why I had trouble getting transportation from the vehicle pool to pick you up."

"I see—" I repeated. I had been about to ask him some more; but just then the door to the control compartment opened behind us and Amanda stepped in.

"Well, Corunna," she said, "how about giving me a chance to talk with Michael?"

She smiled past me at him; and he smiled back. I did not think he had been strongly taken by her—whatever was hidden in him was a barrier to anything like that. But her very presence, with all it implied of home, was plainly warming to him.

"Go ahead," I said, getting up. "I'll go say a word or two to the Outbond."

"He's worth talking to," Amanda spoke after me as I went.

I stepped out, closed the door behind me, and rejoined Padma in the lounge area. He was looking out the window beside him and down at the plains area that lay between the town and the small mountain from which Gebel Nahar took its name. The city we had just left was on a small rise west of that mountain, with suburban and planted areas in between. Around and beyond that mountain—for the fort-like residence that was Gebel Nahar faced east—the actual, open grazing land of the cattle plains began. Our bus was one of those vehicles designed to fly ordinarily at about tree-top level, though of course it could go right up to the limits of the atmosphere in a pinch, but right now we were about three hundred meters up. As I stepped out of the control compartment, Padma took his attention from the window and looked back at me.

"Your Amanda's amazing," he said, as I sat down facing him, "for someone so young."

"She said something like that about you," I told him. "But in her case, she's not quite as young as she looks."

"I know," Padma smiled. "I was speaking from the viewpoint of my own age. To me, even you seem young."

I laughed. What I had had of youth had been far back, some years before Baunpore. But it was true that in terms of years I was not even middle-aged.

"Michael's been telling me that a revolution seems to be brewing here in Nahar," I said to him.

"Yes." He sobered.

"That wouldn't be what brings someone like you to Gebel Nahar?"

His hazel eyes were suddenly amused.

"I thought Amanda was the one with the questions," he said.

"Are you surprised I ask?" I said. "This is an out of the way location for the Outbond to a full planet."

"True." He shook his head. "But the reasons that bring me here are Exotic ones. Which means, I'm afraid, that I'm not free to discuss them."

"But you know about the local movement toward a revolution?"

"Oh, yes." He sat in perfectly relaxed stillness, his hands loosely together in the lap of his robe, light brown against the dark blue. His face was calm and unreadable. "It's part of the overall pattern of events on this world."

"Just this world?"

He smiled back at me.

"Of course," he said gently, "our Exotic science of ontogenetics deals with the interaction of all known human and natural forces, on all the inhabited worlds. But the situation here in Nahar, and specifically the situation at Gebel Nahar, is primarily a result of local, Cetan forces."

"International planetary politics."

"Yes," he said. "Nahar is surrounded by five other principalities, none of which have cattle-raising land like this. They'd all like to have a part or all of this Colony in their control."

"Which ones are backing the revolutionaries?"

He gazed out the window for a moment without speaking. It was a presumptuous thought on my part to imagine that my strange geas, that made people want to tell me private things, would work on an Exotic. But for a moment I had had the familiar feeling that he was about to open up to me.

"My apologies," he said at last. "It may be that in my old age I'm falling into the habit of treating everyone else like—children."

"How old are you, then?"

He smiled.

"Old—and getting older."

"In any case," I said, "you don't have to apologize to me. It'll be an unusual situation when bordering countries don't take sides in a neighbor's revolution."

"Of course," he said. "Actually, all of the five think they have a hand in it on the side of the revolutionaries. Bad as Nahar is, now, it would be a shambles after a successful revolution, with everybody fighting everybody else for different goals. The other principalities all look for a situation in which they can move in and gain. But you're quite right. International politics is always at work, and it's never simple."

"What's fueling this situation, then?"

"William," Padma looked directly at me and for the first time I felt the remarkable effect of his hazel eyes. His face held such a calmness that all his expression seemed to be concentrated in those eyes.

"William?" I asked.

"William of Ceta."

"That's right," I said, remembering. "He owns this world, doesn't he?"

"It's not really correct to say he owns it," Padma said. "He controls most of it—and a great many parts of other worlds. Our present-day version of a merchant prince, in many ways. But he doesn't control everything, even here on Ceta. For example, the Naharese ranchers have always banded together tightly to deal with him; and his best efforts to split them apart and gain a direct authority in Nahar, haven't worked. He controls after a fashion, but only by manipulating the outside conditions that the ranchers have to deal with."

"So he's the one behind the revolution?"

"Yes."

It was plain enough to me that it was William's involvement here that had brought Padma to this backwater section of the planet. The Exotic science of ontogenetics, which was essentially a study of how humans interacted, both as individuals and societies, was something they took very seriously; and William, as one of the movers and shakers of our time would always have his machinations closely watched by them.

"Well, it's nothing to do with us, at any rate," I said, "except as it affects the Graemes' contract."

"Not entirely," he said. "William, like most gifted individuals, knows the advantage of killing two, or even fifty, birds with one stone. He hires a good many mercenaries, directly and indirectly. It would benefit him if events here could lower the Dorsai reputation and the market value of its military individuals."

"I see—" I began; and broke off as the hull of the bus rang suddenly—as if to a sharp blow.

"Down!" I said, pulling Padma to the floor of the vehicle and away from the window beside which we had been sitting. One good thing about Exotics—

they trust you to know your own line of work. He obeyed me instantly and without protest. We waited ... but there was no repetition of the sound.

"What was it?" he asked, after a moment, but without moving from where I had brought him.

"Solid projectile slug. Probably from a heavy hand weapon," I told him. "We've been shot at. Stay down, if you please, Outbond."

I got up myself, staying low and to the center of the bus, and went through the door into the control compartment. Amanda and Michael both looked around at me as I entered, their faces alert.

"Who's out to get us?" I asked Michael.

He shook his head.

"I don't know," he said. "Here in Nahar, it could be anything or anybody. It could be the revolutionaries or simply someone who doesn't like the Dorsai; or someone who doesn't like Exotics—or even someone who doesn't like me. Finally, it could be someone drunk, drugged, or just in a macho mood."

"—who also has a military hand weapon."

"There's that," Michael said. "But everyone in Nahar is armed; and most of them, legitimately or not, own military weapons."

He nodded at the windscreen.

"Anyway, we're almost down," he said.

I looked out. The interlocked mass of buildings that was the government seat called Gebel Nahar was sprawled halfway down from the top of the small mountain, just below us. In the tropical sunlight, it looked like a resort hotel, built on terraces that descended the steep slope. The only difference was that each terrace terminated in a wall, and the lowest of the walls were ramparts of solid fortifications, with heavy weapons emplaced along them. Gebel Nahar, properly garrisoned, should have been able to dominate the countryside against surface troops all the way out to the horizon, at least on this side of the mountain.

"What's the other side like?" I asked.

"Mountaineering cliff—there's heavy weapon emplacements cut out of the rock there, too, and reached by tunnels going clear through the mountain," Michael answered. "The ranchers spared no expense when they built this place. Gallego thinking. They and their families might all have to hole up here, one day."

But a few moments later we were on the poured concrete surface of a vehicle pool. The three of us went back into the body of the bus to rejoin Padma; and Michael let us out of the vehicle. Outside, the parking area was abnormally silent.

"I don't know what's happened—" said Michael as we set foot outside. We three Dorsai had checked, instinctively, ready to retreat back into the bus and take off again if necessary.

A voice shouting from somewhere beyond the ranked flyers and surface vehicles, brought our heads around. There was the sound of running feet, and a moment later a soldier wearing an energy sidearm, but dressed in the green and red Naharese army uniform with band tabs, burst into sight and slid to a halt, panting before us.

"Sir—" he wheezed, in the local dialect of archaic Spanish. "Gone—"

We waited for him to get his breath; after a second, he tried again.

"They've deserted, sir!" he said to Michael, trying to pull himself to attention. "They've gone—all the regiments, everybody!"

"When?" asked Michael.

"Two hours past. It was all planned. Certainly, it was planned. In each group, at the same time, a man stood up. He said that now was the time to desert, to show the *ricones* where the army stood. They all marched out, with their flags, their guns, everything. Look!"

He turned and pointed. We looked. The vehicle pool was on the fifth or sixth level down from the top of the Gebel Nahar. It was possible to see, from this as from any of the other levels, straight out for miles over the plains. Looking now we saw, so far off no other sign was visible, the tiny, occasional twinkles of reflected sunlight, seemingly right on the horizon.

"They are camped out there; waiting for an army they say will come from all the other countries around, to reinforce them and accomplish the revolution."

"Everyone's gone?" Michael's words in Spanish brought the soldier's eyes back to him.

"All but us. The soldiers of your band, sir. We are the Conde's Elite Guard, now."

"Where are the two Dorsai Commanders?"

"In their offices, sir."

"I'll have to go to them right away," said Michael to the rest of us. "Outbond, will you wait in your quarters, or will you come along with us?"

"I'll come," said Padma.

The five of us went across the parking area, between the crowded vehicles and into a maze of corridors. Through these at last we found our way finally to a large suite of offices, where the outward wall of each room was all window. Through the window of the one we were in, we looked out on the plain below, where the distant and all but invisible Naharese regiments were now camped. We found Kensie and Ian Graeme together in one of the inner offices, standing talking before a massive desk large enough to serve as a conference table for a half-dozen people.

They turned as we came in—and once again I was hit by the curious illusion that I usually experienced on meeting these two. It was striking enough whenever I approached one of them. But when the twins were together, as now, the effect was enhanced.

In my own mind I had always laid it to the fact that in spite of their size—and either one is nearly a head taller than I am—they are so evenly proportioned physically that their true dimensions do not register on you until you have something to measure them by. From a distance it is easy to take them for not much more than ordinary height. Then, having unconsciously underestimated them, you or someone else whose size you know approaches them; and it is that individual who seems to change in size as he, or she, or you get close. If it is you, you are very aware of the change. But if it is someone else, you can still seem to shrink somewhat, along with that other person. To feel yourself become smaller in relationship to someone else is a strange sensation, if the phenomenon is entirely subjective.

In this case, the measuring element turned out to be Amanda, who ran to the two brothers the minute we entered the room. Her home, Fal Morgan, was the homestead closest to the Graeme home of Foralie and the three of them had grown up together. As I said, she was not a small woman, but by the time she had reached them and was hugging Kensie, she seemed to have become not only tiny, but fragile; and suddenly—again, as it always does—the room seemed to orient itself about the two Graemes.

I followed her and held out my hand to Ian.

"Corunna!" he said. He was one of the few who still called me by the first of my personal names. His large hand wrapped around mine. His face—so different, yet so like, to his twin brother's—looked down into mine. In truth, they were identical, and yet there was all the difference in the universe between them. Only it was not a physical difference, for all its powerful effect on the eye. Literally, it was that Ian was lightless, and all the bright element that might have been in him was instead in his brother, so that Kensie radiated double the human normal amount of sunny warmth. Dark and light. Night and day. Brother and brother.

And yet, there was a closeness, an identity, between them of a kind that I had never seen in any other two human beings.

"Do you have to go back right away?" Ian was asking me. "Or will you be staying to take Amanda back?"

"I can stay," I said. "My leave-time to the Dorsai wasn't that tight. Can I be of use, here?"

"Yes," Ian said. "You and I should talk. Just a minute, though—"

He turned to greet Amanda in his turn and tell Michael to check and see if the Conde was available for a visit. Michael went out with the soldier who had met us at the vehicle pool. It seemed that Michael and his bandsmen, plus a handful of servants and the Conde himself, added up to the total present population of Gebel Nahar, outside of those in this room. The ramparts were designed to be defended by a handful of people, if necessary; but we had barely more than a handful in the forty members of the regimental band Michael had led, and they were evidently untrained in anything but marching.

We left Kensie with Amanda and Padma. Ian led me into an adjoining office, waved me to a chair, and took one himself.

"I don't know the situation on your present contract—" he began.

"There's no problem. My contract's to a space force leased by William of Ceta. I'm leader of Red Flight under the overall command of Hendrik Galt. Aside from the fact that Galt would understand, as any other Dorsai would, if a situation like this warranted it, his forces aren't doing anything at the moment. Which is why I was on leave in the first place, along with half his other senior officers. I'm not William's officer. I'm Galt's."

"Good," said Ian. He turned his head to look past the high wing of the chair he was sitting in and out over the plain at where the little flashes of light were visible. His arms lay relaxed upon the arms of the chair, his massive hands loosely curved about the ends of those chair arms. There was, as there always had been, something utterly lonely but utterly invincible about Ian. Most non-Dorsais seem to draw a noticeable comfort from having a Dorsai around in times of physical danger, as if they assumed that any one of us would know the right thing to do and so do it. It may sound fanciful, but I have to say that in somewhat the same way as the non-Dorsai reacted to the Dorsai, so did most of the Dorsai I've known always react to Ian.

But not all of us. Kensie never had, of course. Nor, come to think of it, had any of the other Graemes to my knowledge. But then, there had always been something—not solitary, but independent and apart—about each of the Graemes. Even Kensie. It was a characteristic of the family. Only, Ian had that double share of it.

"It'll take them two days to settle in out there," he said now, nodding at the nearly invisible encampments on the plain. "After that, they'll either have to move against us, or they'll start fighting among themselves. That means we can expect to be overrun here in two days."

"Unless what?" I asked. He looked back at me.

"There's always an unless," I said.

"Unless Amanda can find us an honorable way out of the situation," he said. "As it now stands, there doesn't seem to be any way out. Our only hope is that she can find something in the contract or the situation that the rest of us have overlooked. Drink?"

"Thanks."

He got up and went to a sideboard, poured a couple of glasses half-full of dark brown liquor, and brought them back. He sat down once more, handing a glass to me, and I sniffed at its pungent darkness.

"Dorsai whisky," I said. "You're provided for, here."

He nodded. We drank.

"Isn't there anything you think she might be able to use?" I asked.

"No," he said. "It's a hope against hope. An honor problem."

"What makes it so sensitive that you need an Adjuster from home?" I asked.

"William. You know him, of course. But how much do you know about the situation here in Nahar?"

I repeated to him what I had picked up from Michael and Padma.

"Nothing else?" he asked.

"I haven't had time to find out anything else. I was asked to bring Amanda here on the spur of the moment, so on the way out I had my hands full. Also, she was busy studying the available data on this situation herself. We didn't talk much."

"William—" he said, putting his glass down on a small table by his chair. "Well, it's my fault we're

into this, rather than Kensie's. I'm the strategist, he's
the tactician on this contract. The large picture was
my job, and I didn't look far enough."

"If there were things the Naharese government
didn't tell you when the contract was under discus-
sion, then there's your out, right there."

"Oh, the contract's challengeable, all right," Ian
said. He smiled. I know there are those who like to
believe that he never smiles; and that notion is nonsense. But his smile is like all the rest of him. "It
wasn't the information they held back that's trapped
us, it's this matter of honor. Not just our personal
honor—the reputation and honor of all Dorsai.
They've got us in a position where whether we stay
and die or go and live, it'll tarnish the planetary reputation."

I frowned at him.

"How can they do that? How could you get caught
in that sort of trap?"

"Partly," Ian lifted his glass, drank, and put it
back down again, "because William's an extremely
able strategist himself—again, as you know. Partly,
because it didn't occur to me, or Kensie, that we
were getting into a three-party rather than a two-
party agreement."

"I don't follow you."

"The situation in Nahar," he said, "was always
one with its built-in termination clause—I mean, for
the ranchers, the original settlers. The type of country they tried to set up was something that could only
exist under uncrowded, near-pioneering conditions.
The principalities around their grazing area got set-

tled in, some fifty Cetan years ago. After that, the neighboring countries got built up and industrialized; and the semi-feudal notion of open plains and large individual holdings of land got to be impractical, on the international level of this world. Of course, the first settlers, those Gallegos from Galicia in northwest Spain, saw that coming from the start. That was why they built this place we're sitting in."

His smile came again.

"But that was back when they were only trying to delay the inevitable," he said. "Sometime in more recent years they evidently decided to come to terms with it."

"Bargain with the more modern principalities around them, you mean?" I said.

"Bargain with the rest of Ceta, in fact," he said. "And the rest of Ceta, nowadays, is William—for all practical purposes."

"There again, if they had an agreement with William that they didn't tell you about," I said, "you've every excuse, in honor as well as on paper, to void the contract. I don't see the difficulty."

"Their deal they've got with William isn't a written, or even a spoken contract," Ian answered. "What the ranchers did was let him know that he could have the control he wanted here in Nahar—as I said, it was obvious they were going to lose it eventually, anyway—if not to him, to someone or something else—if he'd meet their terms."

"And what were they after in exchange?"

"A guarantee that their life style and this pocket

culture they'd developed would be maintained and protected."

He looked under his dark brows at me.

"I see," I said. "How did they think William could do that?"

"They didn't know. But they didn't worry about it. That's the slippery part. They just let the fact be known to William that if they got what they wanted they'd stop fighting his attempts to control Nahar directly. They left it up to him to find the ways to meet their price. That's why there's no other contract we can cite as an excuse to break this one."

I drank from my own glass.

"It sounds like William. If I know him," I said, "he'd even enjoy engineering whatever situation was needed to keep this country fifty years behind the times. But it sounded to me earlier as if you were saying that he was trying to get something out of the Dorsai at the same time. What good does it do him if you have to make a penalty payment for breaking this contract? It won't bankrupt you Graemes to pay it, will it? And even if you had to borrow from general Dorsai contingency funds, it wouldn't be more than a pinprick against those funds. Also, you still haven't explained this business of your being trapped here, not by the contract, but by the general honor of the Dorsai."

Ian nodded.

"William's taken care of both things," he said. "His plan was for the Naharese to hire Dorsai to make their army a working unit. Then his revolutionary agents would cause a revolt of that army. Then, with matters out of hand, he could step in with his own non-Dorsai officers to control the situation and bring order back to Nahar."

"I see," I said.

"He then would mediate the matter," Ian went on, "the revolutionary people would be handed some limited say in the government—under his outside control, of course—and the ranchers would give up their absolute local authority but little of anything else. They'd stay in charge of their ranches, as his managers, with all his wealth and forces to back them against any real push for control by the real revolutionary faction; which would eventually be tamed and brought in line, also—the way he's tamed and brought in line all the rest of this world, and some good-sized chunks of other worlds."

"So," I said, thoughtfully, "what he's after is to show that his military people can do things Dorsai can't?"

"You follow me," said Ian. "We command the price we do now only because military like ourselves are in limited supply. If they want Dorsai results— military situations dealt with at either no cost or a minimum cost, in life and material—they have to hire Dorsai. That's as it stands now. But if it looks like others can do the same job as well or better, our price has to go down, and the Dorsai will begin to starve."

"It'd take some years for the Dorsai to starve. In that time we could live down the results of this, maybe."

"But it goes farther than that. William isn't the

first to dream of being able to hire all the Dorsai and use them as a personal force to dominate the worlds. We've never considered allowing all our working people to end up in one camp. But if William can depress our price below what we need to keep the Dorsai free and independent, then he can offer us wages better than the market—survival wages, available from him alone—and we'll have no choice but to accept."

"Then you've got no choice, yourself," I said. "You've got to break this contract, no matter what it costs."

"I'm afraid not," he answered. "The cost looks right now to be the one we can't afford to pay. As I said, we're damned if we do, damned if we don't— caught in the jaws of this nutcracker unless Amanda can find us a way out—"

The door to the office where we were sitting opened at that moment and Amanda herself looked in.

"It seems some local people calling themselves the Governors have just arrived—" Her tone was humorous, but every line of her body spoke of serious concern. "Evidently, I'm supposed to go and talk with them right away. Are you coming, Ian?"

"Kensie is all you'll need," Ian said. "We've trained them to realize that they don't necessarily get both of us on deck every time they whistle. You'll find it's just another step in the dance, anyway— there's nothing to be done with them."

"All right." She started to withdraw, stopped. "Can Padma come with us?"

"Check with Kensie. I'd say it's best not to ruffle the Governors' feathers by asking to let him sit in, right now."

"That's all right," she said. "Kensie already thought not, but he said I should ask you."

She went out.

"Sure you don't want to be there?" I asked him.

"No need." He got up. "There's something I want to show you. It's important you understand the situation here thoroughly. If Kensie and myself should both be knocked out, Amanda would only have you to help her handle things—and if you're certain about being able to stay?"

"As I said," I repeated, "I can stay."

"Fine. Come along, then. I wanted you to meet the Conde de Nahar. But I've been waiting to hear from Michael as to whether the Conde's receiving, right now. We won't wait any longer. Let's go see how the old gentleman is."

"Won't he—the Conde, I mean—be at this meeting with Amanda and the Governors?"

Ian led the way out of the room.

"Not if there's serious business to be talked about. On paper, the Conde controls everything but the Governors. They elect him. Of course, aside from the paper, they're the ones who really control everything."

We left the suite of offices and began to travel the corridors of Gebel Nahar once more. Twice we took lift tubes and once we rode a motorized strip down one long corridor; but at the end Ian pushed open a door and we stepped into what was obviously the orderly room fronting a barracks section.

The soldier bandsman seated behind the desk there came to his feet immediately at the sight of us—or perhaps it was just at the sight of Ian.

"Sirs!" he said, in Spanish.

"I ordered Mr. de Sandoval to find out for me if the Conde would receive Captain El Man here, and myself," Ian said in the same language. "Do you know where the Bandmaster is now?"

"No, sir. He has not come back. Sir—it is not always possible to contact the Conde quickly—"

"I'm aware of that," said Ian. "Rest easy. Mr. de Sandoval's due back here shortly, then?"

"Yes, sir. Any minute now. Would the sirs care to wait in the Bandmaster's office?"

"Yes," said Ian.

The orderly turned aside, lifting his hand in a decidedly non-military gesture to usher us past his desk through a farther entrance into a larger room, very orderly and with a clean desk, but crowded with filing cabinets and with its walls hung with musical instruments.

Most of these were ones I had never seen before, although they were all variants on string or wind music-makers. There was one that looked like an early Scottish bagpipe. It had only a single drone, some seventy centimeters long, and a chanter about half that length. Another was obviously a keyed bugle of some sort, but with most of its central body length wrapped with red cord ending in dependent tassels. I moved about the walls, examining each as

I came to it, while Ian took a chair and watched me. I came back at length to the deprived bagpipe.

"Can you play this?" I asked Ian.

"I'm not a piper," said Ian. "I can blow a bit, of course—but I've never played anything but regular highland pipes. You'd better ask Michael if you want a demonstration. Apparently, he plays everything— and plays it well."

I turned away from the walls and took a seat myself.

"What do you think?" asked Ian. I was gazing around the office.

I looked back at him and saw his gaze curiously upon me.

"It's . . . strange," I said.

And the room was strange, for reasons that would probably never strike someone not a Dorsai. No two people keep an office the same way; but just as there are subtle characteristics by which one born to the Dorsai will recognize another, so there are small signals about the office of anyone on military duty and from that world. I could tell at a glance, as could Ian or any one of us, if the officer into whose room we had just stepped was Dorsai or not. The clues lie, not so much with what was in the room, as in the way the things there and the room itself was arranged. There is nothing particular to Dorsai-born individuals about such a recognition. Almost any veteran officer is able to tell you whether the owner of the office he has just stepped into is also a veteran officer, Dorsai or not. But in that case, as in this, it would be easier to give the answer than to list the reasons why the answer was what it was.

So, Michael de Sandoval's office was unmistakably the office of a Dorsai. At the same time it owned a strange difference from any other Dorsai's office, that almost shouted at us. The difference was a basic one, underneath any comparison of this place with the office of a Dorsai who had his walls hung with weapons, or with one who kept a severely clean desktop and message baskets, and preferred no weapon in sight.

"He's got these musical instruments displayed as if they were fighting tools," I said.

Ian nodded. It was not necessary to put the implication into words. If Michael had chosen to hang a banner from one of the walls testifying to the fact that he would absolutely refuse to lay his hands upon a weapon, he could not have announced himself more plainly to Ian and myself.

"It seems to be a strong point with him," I said. "I wonder what happened?"

"His business, of course," said Ian.

"Yes," I said.

But the discovery hurt me—because suddenly I identified what I had felt in young Michael from the first moment I had met him, here on Ceta. It was pain, a deep and abiding pain; and you cannot have known someone since he was in childhood and not be moved by that sort of pain.

The orderly stuck his head into the room.

"Sirs," he said, "the Bandmaster comes. He'll be here in one minute."

"Thank you," said Ian.

A moment later, Michael came in.

"Sorry to keep you waiting—" he began.

"Perfectly all right," Ian said. "The Conde made you wait yourself before letting you speak with him, didn't he?"

"Yes sir."

"Well, is he available now, to be met by me and Captain El Man?"

"Yes sir. You're both most welcome."

"Good."

Ian stood up and so did I. We went out, followed by Michael to the door of his office.

"Amanda Morgan is seeing the Governors, at the moment," Ian said to him as we left him. "She may want to talk to you after that's over. You might keep yourself available for her."

"I'll be right here," said Michael. "Sir—I wanted to apologize for my orderly's making excuses about my not being here when you came—" he glanced over at the orderly who was looking embarrassed. "My men have been told not to—"

"It's all right, Michael," said Ian. "You'd be an unusual Dorsai if they didn't try to protect you."

"Still—" said Michael.

"Still," said Ian. "I know they've trained only as bandmen. They may be line troops at the moment— all the line troops we've got to hold this place with— but I'm not expecting miracles."

"Well," said Michael. "Thank you, Commander."

"You're welcome."

We went out. Once more Ian led me through a maze of corridors and lifts.

"How many of his band decided to stay with him when the regiments moved out?" I asked as we went.

"All of them," said Ian.

"And no one else stayed?"

Ian looked at me with a glint of humor.

"You have to remember," he said, "Michael did graduate from the Academy, after all."

A final short distance down a wide corridor brought us to a massive pair of double doors. Ian touched a visitor's button on the right-hand door and spoke to an annunciator panel in Spanish.

"Commander Ian Graeme and Captain El Man are here with permission to see the Conde."

There was the pause of a moment and then one of the doors opened to show us another of Michael's bandsmen.

"Be pleased to come in, sirs," he said.

"Thank you," Ian said as we walked past. "Where's the Conde's majordomo?"

"He is gone, sir. Also most of the other servants."

"I see."

The room we had just been let into was a wide lobby filled with enormous and magnificently-kept furniture but lacking any windows. The bandman led us through two more rooms like it, also without windows, until we were finally ushered into a third and finally window-walled room, with the same unchanging view of the plains below. A stick-thin old man dressed in black was standing with the help of a silver-headed cane, before the center of the window area.

The soldier faded out of the room. Ian led me to the old man.

"El Conde," he said, still in Spanish, "may I introduce Captain Corunna El Man. Captain, you have the honor of meeting El Conde de Nahar, Macias Francisco Ramón Manuel Valentin y Compostela y Abente."

"You are welcome, Captain El Man," said the Conde. He spoke a more correct, if more archaic, Spanish than that of the other Naharese I had so far met; and his voice was the thin remnant of what once must have been a remarkable bass. "We will sit down now, if you please. If my age produces a weakness, it is that it is wearisome to stand for any length of time."

We settled ourselves in heavy, overstuffed chairs with massively padded arms—more like thrones than chairs.

"Captain El Man," said Ian, "happened to be on leave, back on the Dorsai. He volunteered to bring Amanda Morgan here to discuss the present situation with the Governors. She's talking to them now."

"I have not met . . ." the Conde hesitated over her name, "Amanda Morgan."

"She is one of our experts of the sort that the present situation calls for."

"I would like to meet her."

"She's looking forward to meeting you."

"Possibly this evening? I would have liked to have

had all of you to dinner, but you know, I suppose, that most of my servants have gone."

"I just learned that," said Ian.

"They may go," said the Conde. "They will not be allowed to return. Nor will the regiments who have deserted their duty be allowed to return to my armed forces."

"With the Conde's indulgence," said Ian, "we don't yet know all the reasons for their leaving. It may be that some leniency is justified."

"I can think of none." The Conde's voice was thin with age, but his back was as erect as a flagstaff and his dark eyes did not waver. "But, if you think there is some reason for it, I can reserve judgment momentarily."

"We'd appreciate that," Ian said.

"You are very lenient." The Conde looked at me. His voice took on an unexpected timbre. "Captain, has the Commander here told you? Those deserters out there—" he flicked a finger toward the window and the plains beyond, "under the instigation of people calling themselves revolutionaries, have threatened to take over Gebel Nahar. If they dare to come here, I and what few loyal servants remain will resist. To the death!"

"The Governors—" Ian began.

"The Governors have nothing to say in the matter!" the Conde turned fiercely on him. "Once, they—their fathers and grandfathers, rather—chose my father to be El Conde. I inherited that title and neither they, nor anyone else in the universe has the authority to take it from me. While I live, I will be El Conde; and the only way I will cease to be El Conde will be when death takes me. I will remain, I will fight—alone if need be—as long as I am able. But I will retreat, never! I will compromise, *never!*"

He continued to talk, for some minutes; but although his words changed, the message of them remained the same. He would not give an inch to anyone who wished to change the governmental system in Nahar. If he had been obviously uninformed or ignorant of the implications of what he was saying, it would have been easy to let his words blow by unheeded. But this was obviously not the case. His frailty was all in the thin old body. His mind was not only clear but fully aware of the situation. What he announced was simply an unshakable determination never to yield in spite of reason or the overwhelming odds against him.

After a while he ran down. He apologized graciously for his emotion, but not for his attitude; and, after a few minutes more of meaninglessly polite conversation on the history of Gebel Nahar itself, let us leave.

"So you see part of our problem," said Ian to me when we were alone again, walking back to his offices.

We went a little distance together in silence.

"Part of that problem," I said, "seems to lie in the difference between our idea of honor, and theirs, here."

"And William's complete lack of it," said Ian. "You're right. With us, honor's a matter of the individual's obligation to himself and his community—

which can end up being to the human race in general. To the Naharese, honor's an obligation only to their own soul."

I laughed, involuntarily.

"I'm sorry," I said, as he looked at me. "But you hit it almost too closely. Did you ever read Calderón's poem about the Mayor of Zalamea?"

"I don't think so. Calderón?"

"Pedro Calderón de la Barca, seventeenth century Spanish poet. He wrote a poem called *El Alcalde de Zalamea*."

I gave him the lines he had reminded me of.

> *Al Rey la hacienda y la vida*
> *Se ha de dar; pero el honor*
> *Es patrimonio del alma*
> *Y el alma soló es de Dios.*

" '—*Fortune and life we owe to the King,*' " murmured Ian, " '*but honor is patrimony of the soul and the soul belongs to God alone.*' I see what you mean."

I started to say something, then decided it was too much effort. I was aware of Ian glancing sideways at me as we went.

"When did you eat last?" he asked.

"I don't remember," I said. "But I don't particularly need food right now."

"You need sleep, then," said Ian, "I'm not surprised, after the way you made it here from the Dorsai. When we get back to the office, I'll call one of Michael's men to show you your quarters, and

you'd better sleep in. I can make your excuses to the
Conde if he still wants us to get together tonight."

"Yes. Good," I said. "I'd appreciate that."

Now that I had admitted to tiredness, it was an
effort even to think. For those who have never nav-
igated between the stars, it is easy to forget the implications in the fact that the danger increases rapidly
with the distance moved in a single shift—beyond a
certain safe amount of light-years. We had exceeded
safe limits as far as I had dared push them on each
of the six shifts that had brought Amanda and myself
to Ceta.

It's not just that danger—the danger of finding
yourself with so large an error in destination that you
cannot recognize any familiar star patterns from
which to navigate. It is the fact that even when you
emerge in known space, a large error factor requires
infinitely more recalculation to locate your position.
It is vital to locate yourself to a fine enough point so
that your error on the next shift will not be com-
pounded and you will find yourself lost beyond re-
pair.

For three days I had had no more than catnaps
between periods of calculation. I was numb with a
fatigue I had held at bay until this moment with the
body adrenalin that can be evoked to meet an emergency situation.

When the bandsman supplied by Ian had shown
me at last to a suite of rooms, I found I wanted nothing more than to collapse on the enormous bed in the
bedroom. But years of instinct made me prowl the
quarters first and check them out. My suite consisted

of three rooms and bathroom; and it had the inevitable plains-facing window wall—with one difference. This one had a door in it to let me out onto a small balcony that ran the length of this particular level. It was divided into a semi-private outdoor area for each suite by tall plants in pots which acted as screens at each division point.

I checked the balcony area and the suite, locked the doors to the hall and to the balcony, and slept.

It was sometime after dark when I awoke, suddenly. I was awake and sitting up on the edge of the bed in one reflex movement before it registered that what had roused me had been the sound of the call chime at the front door of my suite.

I reached over and keyed on the annunciator circuit.

"Yes?" I said. "Who is it?"

"Michael de Sandoval," said Michael's voice, "can I come in?"

I touched the stud that unlocked the door. It swung open, letting a knife-blade sharp swath of light from the corridor into the darkness of my sitting room, as seen through the entrance from my bedroom. I was up on my feet now, and moving to meet him in the sitting room. He entered and the door closed behind him.

"What is it?" I asked.

"The ventilating system is out on this level," he said; and I realized that the air in the suite was now perfectly motionless—motionless and beginning to be a little warm and stuffy. Evidently Gebel Nahar had been designed to be sealed against outside atmosphere.

"I wanted to check the quarters of everyone on this level," Michael said. "Interior doors aren't so tight that you would have asphyxiated; but the breathing could have got a little heavy. Maybe by morning we can locate what's out of order and fix it. This is part of the problem of the servant staff taking off when the army did. I'd suggest that I open the door to the balcony for you, sir."

He was already moving across the room toward the door he had mentioned.

"Thanks," I said. "What was the situation with the servants? Were they revolutionary sympathizers, too?"

"Not necessarily." He unlocked the door and propped it open to the night air, which came coolly and sweetly through the aperture. "They just didn't want their throats cut along with the Conde's, when the army stormed its way back in here."

"I see," I said.

"Yes." He came back to me in the center of the sitting room.

"What time is it?" I asked. "I've been sleeping as if I was under drugs."

"A little before midnight."

I sat down in one of the chairs of the unlighted lounge. The glow of the soft exterior lights spaced at ten meter intervals along the outer edge of the balcony came through the window wall and dimly illuminated the room.

"Sit for a moment," I said. "Tell me. How did the meeting with the Conde go this evening?"

He took a chair facing me.

"I should be getting back soon," he said. "I'm the only one we've got available for a duty officer at the moment. But—the meeting with the Conde went like a charm. He was so busy being gracious to Amanda he almost forgot to breathe defiance against the army deserters."

"How did Amanda do with the Governors, do you know?"

I sensed, rather than saw, a shrug of his shoulders in the gloom.

"There was nothing much to be done with them," he said. "They talked about their concern over the desertion of the regiments and wanted reassurances that Ian and Kensie could handle the situation. Effectively, it was all choreographed."

"They've left, then?"

"That's right. They asked for guarantees for the safety of the Conde. Both Ian and Kensie told them that there was no such thing as a guarantee; but we'd protect the Conde, of course, with every means at our disposal. Then they left."

"It sounds," I said, "as if Amanda could have saved her time and effort."

"No. She said she wanted to get the feel of them." He leaned forward. "You know, she's something to write home about. I think if anyone can find a way out of this, she can. She says herself that there's no question that there is a way out—it's just that finding it in the next twenty-four to thirty-six hours is asking a lot."

"Has she checked with you about these people? You seem to be the only one around who knows them at all well."

"She talked with me when we flew in—you remember. I told her I'd be available any time she needed me. So far, however, she's spent most of her time either working by herself, or with Ian or Padma."

"I see," I said. "Is there anything I can do? Would you like me to spell you on the duty officer bit?"

"You're to rest, Ian says. He'll need you tomorrow. I'm getting along fine with my duties." He moved toward the front door of the suite. "Good night."

"Good night," I said.

He went out, the knife of light from the corridor briefly cutting across the carpeting of my sitting room and vanishing again as the door opened, then latched behind him.

I stayed where I was in the sitting room chair, enjoying the gentle night breeze through the propped-open door. I may have dozed. At any rate I came to, suddenly, to the sound of voices from the balcony. Not from my portion of the balcony, but from the portion next to it, beyond my bedroom window to the left.

"... yes," a voice was saying. Ian had been in my mind; and for a second I thought I was hearing Ian speak. But it was Kensie. The voices were identical;

only, there was a difference in attitude that distinguished them.

"I don't know . . ." it was Amanda's voice answering, a troubled voice.

"Time goes by quickly," Kensie said. "Look at us. It was just yesterday we were in school together."

"I know," she said, "You're talking about it being time to settle down. But maybe I never will."

"How sure are you of that?"

"Not sure, of course." Her voice changed as if she had moved some little distance from him. I had an unexpected mental image of him standing back by the door in a window wall through which they had just come out together; and one of her, having just turned and walked to the balcony railing, where she now stood with her back to him, looking out at the night and the starlit plain.

"Then you could take the idea of settling down under consideration."

"No," she said. "I know I don't want to do that." Her voice changed again, as if she had turned and come back to him. "Maybe I'm ghost-ridden, Kensie. Maybe it's the old spirit of the first Amanda that's ruling out the ordinary things for me."

"She married—three times."

"But her husbands weren't important to her, that way. Oh, I know she loved them. I've read her letters and what her children wrote down about her after they were adults themselves. But she really belonged to everyone, not just to her husbands and children. Don't you understand? I think that's the way it's going to have to be for me, too."

He said nothing. After a long moment she spoke again, and her voice was lowered, and drastically altered.

"Kensie! Is it that important?"

His voice was lightly humorous, but the words came a fraction more slowly than they had before.

"It seems to be."

"But it's something we both just fell into, as children. It was just an assumption on both our parts. Since then, we've grown up. You've changed. I've changed."

"Yes."

"You don't need me. Kensie, you don't need *me*—" her voice was soft. "Everybody loves you."

"Could I trade?" The humorous tone persisted. "Everybody for you?"

"Kensie, don't!"

"You ask a lot," he said; and now the humor was gone, but there was still nothing in the way he spoke that reproached her. "I'd probably find it easier to stop breathing."

There was another silence.

"Why can't you see? I don't have any other choice," she said. "I don't have any more choice than you do. We're both what we are, and stuck with what we are."

"Yes," he said.

The silence this time lasted a long time. But they did not move, either of them. By this time my ear was sensitized to sounds as light as the breathing of a sparrow. They had been standing a little apart, and they stayed standing apart.

"Yes," he said again, finally—and this time it was a long, slow *yes*, a tired *yes*. "Life moves. And all of us move with it, whether we like it or not."

She moved to him, now. I heard her steps on the concrete floor of the balcony.

"You're exhausted," she said. "You and Ian both. Get some rest before tomorrow. Things'll look different in the daylight."

"That sometimes happens." The touch of humor was back, but there was effort behind it. "Not that I believe it for a moment, in this case."

They went back inside.

I sat where I was, wide awake. There had been no way for me to get up and get away from their conversation without letting them know I was there. Their hearing was at least as good as mine, and like me they had been trained to keep their senses always alert. But knowing all that did not help. I still had the ugly feeling that I had been intruding where I should not have been.

There was no point in moving now. I sat where I was, trying to talk sense to myself and get the ugly feeling under control. I was so concerned with my own feelings that for once I did not pay close attention to the sounds around me, and the first warning I had was a small noise in my own entrance to the balcony area; and I looked up to see the dark silhouette of a woman in the doorway.

"You heard," Amanda's voice said.

There was no point in denying it.

"Yes," I told her.

She stayed where she was, standing in the doorway.

"I happened to be sitting here when you came out on the balcony," I said. "There was no chance to shut the door or move away."

"It's all right," she came in. "No, don't turn on the light."

I dropped the hand I had lifted toward the control studs in the arm of my chair. With the illumination from the balcony behind her, she could see me better than I could see her. She sat down in the chair Michael had occupied a short while before.

"I told myself I'd step over and see if you were sleeping all right," she said. "Ian has a lot of work in mind for you tomorrow. But I think I was really hoping to find you awake.

Even through the darkness, the signals came loud and clear. My geas was at work again.

"I don't want to intrude," I said.

"If I reach out and haul you in by the scruff of the neck, are you intruding?" Her voice had the same sort of lightness overlying pain that I had heard in Kensie's. "I'm the one who's thinking of intruding—of intruding my problems on you."

"That's not necessarily an intrusion," I said.

"I hoped you'd feel that way," she said. It was strange to have her voice coming in such everyday tones from a silhouette of darkness. "I wouldn't bother you, but I need to have all my mind on what I'm doing here and personal matters have ended up getting in the way."

She paused.

"You don't really mind people spilling all over you, do you?" she said.

"No," I said.

"I thought so. I got the feeling you wouldn't. Do you think of Else much?"

"When other things aren't on my mind."

"I wish I'd known her."

"She was someone to know."

"Yes. Knowing someone else is what makes the difference. The trouble is, often we don't know. Or we don't know until too late." She paused. "I suppose you think after what you heard just now, that I'm talking about Kensie?"

"Aren't you?"

"No. Kensie and Ian—the Graemes are so close to us Morgans that we might as well all be related. You don't usually fall in love with a relative—or you don't think you will, at least, when you're young. The kind of person you imagine falling in love with is someone strange and exciting—someone from fifty light years away."

"I don't know about that," I said. "Else was a neighbor and I think I grew up being in love with her."

"I'm sorry." Her silhouette shifted a little in the darkness. "I'm really just talking about myself. But I know what you mean. In sober moments, when I was younger, I more or less assumed that some day I'd wind up with Kensie. You'd have to have something wrong with you not to want someone like him."

"And you've got something wrong with you?" I said.

"Yes," she said. "That's it. I grew up, that's the trouble."

"Everybody does."

"I don't mean I grew up, physically. I mean, I matured. We live a long time, we Morgans, and I suppose we're slower growing up than most. But you know how it is with young anythings—young animals as well as young humans. Did you ever have a wild animal as a pet as a child?"

"Several," I said.

"Then you've run into what I'm talking about. While the wild animal's young, it's cuddly and tame; but when it grows up, the day comes it bites or slashes at you without warning. People talk about that being part of their wild nature. But it isn't. Humans change just exactly the same way. When anything young grows up, it becomes conscious of itself, its own wants, its own desires, its own moods. Then the day comes when someone tries to play with it and it isn't in a playing mood—and it reacts with *'Back off! What I want is just as important as what you want!'* And all at once, the time of its being young and cuddly is over forever."

"Of course," I said. "That happens to all of us."

"But to us—to our people—it happens too late!" she said. "Or rather, we start life too early. By the age of seventeen on the Dorsai we have to be out and working like an adult, either at home or on some other world. We're pitchforked into adulthood. There's never any time to take stock, to realize what being adult is going to turn us into. We don't realize we aren't cubs any more until one day we slash or bite someone without warning; and then we realize that we've changed—and they've changed. But it's too late for us to adjust to the change in the other person because we've already been trapped by our own change."

She stopped. I sat, not speaking, waiting. From my experience with this sort of thing since Else died, I assumed that I no longer needed to talk. She would carry the conversation, now.

"No, it wasn't Kensie I was talking about when I first came in here and I said the trouble is you don't know someone else until too late. It's Ian."

"Ian?" I said, for she had stopped again, and now I felt with equal instinct that she needed some help to continue.

"Yes," she said. "When I was young, I didn't understand Ian. I do now. Then, I thought there was nothing to him—or else he was simply solid all the way through, like a piece of wood. But he's not. Everything you can see in Kensie is there in Ian, only there's no light to see it by. Now I know. And now it's too late."

"Too late?" I said. "He's not married, is he?"

"Married? Not yet. But you didn't know? Look at the picture on his desk. Her name's Leah. She's on Earth. He met her when he was there, four years ago. But that's not what I mean by too late. I mean—it's too late for me. What you heard me tell Kensie is the truth. I've got the curse of the first Amanda. I'm born to belong to a lot of people, first; and only to any single person, second. As much as I'd give for Ian, that equation's there in me, ever since I grew up.

Sooner or later it'd put even him in second place for me. I can't do that to him; and it's too late for me to be anything else."

"Maybe Ian'd be willing to agree to those terms."

She did not answer for a second. Then I heard a slow intake of breath from the darker darkness that was her.

"You shouldn't say that," she said.

There was a second of silence. Then she spoke again, fiercely.

"Would you suggest something like that to Ian if our positions were reversed?"

"I didn't suggest it," I said. "I mentioned it."

Another pause.

"You're right," she said. "I know what I want and what I'm afraid of in myself, and it seems to me so obvious I keep thinking everyone else must know too."

She stood up.

"Forgive me, Corunna," she said. "I've got no right to burden you with all this."

"It's the way the world is," I said. "People talk to people."

"And to you, more than most." She went toward the door to the balcony and paused in it. "Thanks again."

"I've done nothing," I said.

"Thank you anyway. Good night. Sleep if you can."

She stepped out through the door; and through the window wall I watched her, very erect, pass to my left until she walked out of my sight beyond the sitting room wall.

I went back to bed, not really expecting to fall asleep again easily. But I dropped off and slept like a log.

When I woke it was morning, and my bedside phone was chiming. I flicked it on and Michael looked at me out of the screen.

"I'm sending a man up with maps of the interior of Gebel Nahar," he said, "so you can find your way around. Breakfast's available in the General Staff Lounge, if you're ready."

"Thanks," I told him.

I got up and was ready when the bandsman he had sent arrived, with a small display cube holding the maps. I took it with me and the bandsman showed me to the General Staff Lounge—which, it turned out, was not a lounge for the staff of Gebel Nahar, in general, but one for the military commanders of that establishment. Ian was the only other present when I got there and he was just finishing his meal.

"Sit down," he said.

I sat.

"I'm going ahead on the assumption that I'll be defending this place in twenty-four hours or so," he said. "What I'd like you to do is familiarize yourself with its defenses, particularly the first line of walls and its weapons, so that you can either direct the men working them, or take over the general defense, if necessary."

"What have you got in mind for a general defense?" I asked, as a bandsman came out of the kitchen area to see what I would eat. I told him and he went.

"We've got just about enough of Michael's troops to man that first wall and have a handful in reserve," he said. "Most of them have never touched anything but a handweapon in their life, but we've got to use them to fight with the emplaced energy weapons against foot attack up the slope. I'd like you to get them on the weapons and drill them—Michael should be able to help you, since he knows which of them are steady and which aren't. Get breakfast in you; and I'll tell you what I expect the regiments to do on the attack and what I think we might do when they try it."

He went on talking while my food came and I ate. Boiled down, his expectations—based on what he had learned of the Naharese military while he had been here, and from consultation with Michael— were for a series of infantry wave attacks up the slope until the first wall was overrun. His plan called for a defense of the first wall until the last safe moment, destruction of the emplaced weapons, so they could not be turned against us, and a quick retreat to the second wall with its weapons—and so, step by step retreating up the terraces. It was essentially the sort of defense that Gebel Nahar had been designed for by its builders.

The problem would be getting absolutely green and excitable troops like the Naharese bandsmen to retreat cool-headedly on order. If they could not be brought to do that, and lingered behind, then the first wave over the ramparts could reduce their numbers to the point where there would not be enough of them to make any worthwhile defense of the second terrace, to say nothing of the third, the fourth, and so on, and still have men left for a final stand within the fortress-like walls of the top three levels.

Given an equal number of veteran, properly trained troops, to say nothing of Dorsai-trained ones, we might even have held Gebel Nahar in that fashion and inflicted enough casualties on the attackers to eventually make them pull back. But unspoken between Ian and myself as we sat in the lounge, was the fact that the most we could hope to do with what we had was inflict a maximum of damage while losing.

However, again unspoken between us, was the fact that the stiffer our defense of Gebel Nahar, even in a hopeless situation, the more difficult it would be for the Governors and William to charge the Dorsai officers with incompetence of defense.

I finished eating and got up to go.

"Where's Amanda?" I asked.

"She's working with Padma—or maybe I should put it that Padma's working with her," Ian said.

"I didn't know Exotics took sides."

"He isn't," Ian said. "He's just making knowledge—his knowledge—available to someone who needs it. That's standard Exotic practice as you know as well as I do. He and Amanda are still hunting some political angle to bring us and the Dorsai out of this without prejudice."

"What do you really think their chances are?"

Ian shook his head.

"But," he said, shuffling together the papers he had spread out before him on the lounge table, "of course, where they're looking is away out, beyond the areas of strategy I know. We can hope."

"Did you ever stop to think that possibly Michael, with his knowledge of these Naharese, could give them some insights they wouldn't otherwise have?" I asked.

"Yes," he said. "I told them both that; and told Michael to make himself available to them if they thought they could use him. So far, I don't think they have."

He got up, holding his papers and we went out; I to the band quarters and Michael's office, he to his own office and the overall job of organizing our supplies and everything else necessary for the defense.

Michael was not in his office. The orderly directed me to the first wall, where I found him already drilling his men on the emplaced weapons there. I worked with him for the most of the morning; and then we stopped, not because there was not a lot more practice needed, but because his untrained troops were exhausted and beginning to make mistakes simply out of fatigue.

Michael sent them to lunch. He and I went back to his office and had sandwiches and coffee brought in by his orderly.

"What about this?" I asked, after we were done, getting up and going to the wall where the archaic-looking bagpipe hung. "I asked Ian about it. But he said he'd only played highland pipes and that if I wanted a demonstration, I should ask you."

Michael looked up from his seat behind his desk, and grinned. The drill on the guns seemed to have done something for him in a way he was not really aware of himself. He looked younger and more cheerful than I had yet seen him; and obviously he enjoyed any attention given to his instruments.

"That's a *gaita gallega*," he said. "Or, to be correct, it's a local imitation of the gaita gallega you can still find occasionally being made and played in the province of Galicia in Spain, back on Earth. It's a perfectly playable instrument to anyone who's familiar with the highland pipes. Ian could have played it—I'd guess he just thought I might prefer to show it off myself."

"He seemed to think you could play it better," I said.

"Well . . ." Michael grinned again. "Perhaps, a bit."

He got up and came over to the wall with me.

"Do you really want to hear it?" he asked.

"Yes, I do."

He took it down from the wall.

"We'll have to step outside," he said. "It's not the sort of instrument to be played in a small room like this."

We went back out on to the first terrace by the deserted weapon emplacements. He swung the pipe up in his arms, the long single drone with its fringe tied at the two ends of the drone, resting on his left shoulder and pointing up into the air behind him. He took the mouthpiece between his lips and laid his fingers across the holes of the chanter. Then he blew up the bag and began to play.

The music of the pipes is like Dorsai whisky. People either cannot stand it, or they feel that there's nothing comparable. I happen to be one of those who love the sound—for no good reason, I would have said until that trip to Gebel Nahar; since my own heritage is Spanish rather than Scottish and I had never before realized that it was also a Spanish instrument.

Michael played something Scottish and standard— *The Flowers of the Forest*, I think—pacing slowly up and down as he played. Then, abruptly he swung around and stepped out, almost strutted, in fact; and played something entirely different.

I wish there were words in me to describe it. It was anything but Scottish. It was hispanic, right down to its backbones—a wild, barbaric, musically ornate challenge of some sort that heated the blood in my veins and threatened to raise the hair on the back of my neck.

He finished at last with a sort of dying wail as he swung the deflating bag down from his shoulder. His face was not young any more, it was changed. He looked drawn and old.

"What was that?" I demanded.

"It's got a polite name for polite company," he said. "But nobody uses it. The Naharese call it *Su Madre*."

"Your Mother?" I echoed. Then, of course, it hit me. The Spanish language has a number of elaborate and poetically insulting curses to throw at your en-

emy about his ancestry; and the words *su madre* are found in most of them.

"Yes," said Michael. "It's what you play when you're daring the enemy to come out and fight. It accuses him of being less than a man in all the senses of that phrase—and the Naharese love it."

He sat down on the rampart of the terrace, sud-. denly, like someone very tired and discouraged by a long and hopeless effort, resting the gaita gallega on his knees.

"And they like me," he said, staring blindly at the wall of the barrack area, behind me. "My bandsmen, my regiment—they like me."

"There're always exceptions," I said, watching him. "But usually the men who serve under them like their Dorsai officers."

"That's not what I mean." He was still staring at the wall. "I've made no secret here of the fact I won't touch a weapon. They all knew it from the day I signed on as bandmaster."

"I see," I said. "So that's it."

He looked up at me, abruptly.

"Do you know how they react to cowards—as they consider them—people who are able to fight but won't, in this particular crazy splinter culture? They encourage them to get off the face of the earth. They show their manhood by knocking cowards around here. But they don't touch me. They don't even challenge me to duels."

"Because they don't believe you," I said.

"That's it." His face was almost savage. "They don't. Why won't they believe me?"

"Because you only *say* you won't use a weapon," I told him bluntly. "In every other language you speak, everything you say or do, you broadcast just the opposite information. That tells them that not only can you use a weapon, but that you're so good at it none of them who'd challenge you would stand a chance. You could not only defeat someone like that, you could make him look foolish in the process. And no one wants to look foolish, particularly a macho-minded individual. That message is in the very way you walk and talk. How else could it be, with you?"

"That's not true!" he got suddenly to his feet, holding the gaita. "I live what I believe in. I have, ever since—"

He stopped.

"Maybe we'd better get back to work," I said, as gently as I could.

"No!" The word burst out of him. "I want to tell someone. The odds are we're not going to be around after this. I want someone to . . ."

He broke off. He had been about to say "someone to understand . . ." and he had not been able to get the words out. But I could not help him. As I've said, since Else's death, I've grown accustomed to listening to people. But there is something in me that tells me when to speak and when not to help them with what they wish to say. And now I was being held silent.

He struggled with himself for a few seconds, and then calm seemed to flow over him.

"No," he said, as if talking to himself, "what peo-

ple think doesn't matter. We're not likely to live
through this, and I want to know how you react."

He looked at me.

"That's why I've got to explain it to someone like
you," he said. "I've got to know how they'd take it,
back home, if I'd explained it to them. And your
family is the same as mine, from the same canton,
the same neighborhood, the same sort of ancestry . . ."

"Did it occur to you you might not owe anyone an
explanation?" I said. "When your parents raised you,
they only paid back the debt they owed their parents
for raising them. If you've got any obligation to anyone—and even that's a moot point, since the idea
behind our world is that it's a planet of free people—
it's to the Dorsai in general, to bring in interstellar
exchange credits by finding work off-planet. And
you've done that by becoming bandmaster here.
Anything beyond that's your own private business."

It was quite true. The vital currency between
worlds was not wealth, as every schoolchild knows,
but the exchange of interplanetary work credits. The
inhabited worlds trade special skills and knowledges,
packaged in human individuals; and the exchange
credits earned by a Dorsai on Newton enables the
Dorsai to hire a geophysicist from Newton—or a physician from Kultis. In addition to his personal pay,
Michael had been earning exchange credits ever since
he had come here. True, he might have earned these
at a higher rate if he had chosen work as a mercenary
combat officer; but the exchange credits he did earn

as bandmaster more than justified the expense of his education and training.

"I'm not talking about that—" he began.

"No," I said, "you're talking about a point of obligation and honor not very much removed from the sort of thing these Naharese have tied themselves up with."

He stood for a second, absorbing that. But his mouth was tight and his jaw set.

"What you're telling me," he said at last, "is that you don't want to listen. I'm not surprised."

"Now," I said, "you really are talking like a Naharese. I'll listen to anything you want to say, of course."

"Then sit down," he said.

He gestured to the rampart and sat down himself. I came and perched there, opposite him.

"Do you know I'm a happy man?" he demanded. "I really am. Why not? I've got everything I want. I've got a military job, I'm in touch with all the things that I grew up feeling made the kind of life one of my family ought to have. I'm one of a kind. I'm better at what I do and everything connected with it than anyone else they can find—and I've got my other love, which was music, as my main duty. My men like me, my regiment is proud of me. My superiors like me."

I nodded.

"But then there's this other part . . ." His hands closed on the bag of the gaita, and there was a faint sound from the drone.

"Your refusal to fight?"

"Yes." He got up from the ramparts and began to pace back and forth, holding the instrument, talking a little jerkily. "This feeling against hurting anything ... I had it, too, just as long as I had the other—all the dreams I made up as a boy from the stories the older people in the family told me. When I was young it didn't seem to matter to me that the feeling and the dreams hit head on. It just always happened that, in my own personal visions the battles I won were always bloodless, the victories always came with no one getting hurt. I didn't worry about any conflict in me, then. I thought it was something that would take care of itself later, as I grew up. You don't kill anyone when you're going through the Academy, of course. You know as well as I do that the better you are, the less of a danger you are to your fellow-students. But what was in me didn't change. It was there with me all the time, not changing."

"No normal person likes the actual fighting and killing," I said. "What sets us Dorsai off in a class by ourselves is the fact that most of the time we *can* win bloodlessly, where someone else would have dead bodies piled all over the place. Our way justifies itself to our employers by saving them money; but it also gets us away from the essential brutality of combat and keeps us human. No good officer pins medals on himself in proportion to the people he kills and wounds. Remember what Cletus says about that? He hated what you hate, just as much."

"But he could do it when he had to," Michael stopped and looked at me with a face, the skin of which was drawn tight over the bones. "So can you, now. Or Ian. Or Kensie."

That was true, of course. I could not deny it.

"You see," said Michael, "that's the difference between out on the worlds and back at the Academy. In life, sooner or later, you get to the killing part. Sooner or later, if you live by the sword, you kill with the sword. When I graduated and had to face going out to the worlds as a fighting officer, I finally had to make that decision. And so I did. I can't hurt anyone. I won't hurt anyone—even to save my own life, I think. But at the same time I'm a soldier and nothing else. I'm bred and born a soldier. I don't want any other life, I can't conceive of any other life; and I love it."

He broke off, abruptly. For a long moment he stood, staring out over the plains at the distant flashes of light from the camp of the deserted regiments.

"Well, there it is," he said.

"Yes," I said.

He turned to look at me.

"Will you tell my family that?" he asked. "If you should get home and I don't?"

"If it comes to that, I will," I said. "But we're a long way from being dead, yet."

He grinned, unexpectedly, a sad grin.

"I know," he said. "It's just that I've had this on my conscience for a long time. You don't mind?"

"Of course not."

"Thanks," he said.

He hefted the gaita in his hands as if he had just suddenly remembered that he held it.

"My men will be back out here in about fifteen minutes," he said. "I can carry on with the drilling myself, if you've got other things you want to do."

I looked at him a little narrowly.

"What you're trying to tell me," I said, "is that they'll learn faster if I'm not around."

"Something like that." He laughed. "They're used to me; but you make them self-conscious. They tighten up and keep making the same mistakes over and over again; and then they get into a fury with themselves and do even worse. I don't know if Ian would approve, but I do know these people; and I think I can bring them along faster alone ..."

"Whatever works," I said. "I'll go and see what else Ian can find for me to do."

I turned and went to the door that would let me back into the interior of Gebel Nahar.

"Thank you again," he called after me. There was a note of relief in his voice that moved me more strongly than I had expected, so that instead of telling him that what I had done in listening to him was nothing at all, I simply waved at him and went inside.

I found my way back to Ian's office, but he was not there. It occurred to me, suddenly, that Kensie, Padma or Amanda might know where he had gone—and they should all be at work in other offices of that same suite.

I went looking, and found Kensie with his desk covered with large scale printouts of terrain maps.

"Ian?" He said. "No, I don't know. But he ought to be back in his office soon. I'll have some work for you tonight, by the way. I want to mine the approach slope. Michael's bandsmen can do the actual work, after they've had some rest from the day; but you and I are going to need to go out first and make a sweep to pick up any observers they've sent from the regiments to camp outside our walls. Then later, before dawn I'd like some of us to do a scout of that camp of theirs on the plains and get some hard ideas as to how many of them there are, what they have to attack with, and so on . . ."

"Fine," I said. "I'm all slept up now, myself. Call on me when you want me."

"You could try asking Amanda or Padma if they know where Ian is."

"I was just going to."

Amanda and Padma were in a conference room two doors down from Kensie's office, seated at one end of a long table covered with text printouts and with an activated display screen flat in its top. Amanda was studying the screen and they both looked up as I put my head in the door. But while Padma's eyes were sharp and questioning, Amanda's were abstract, like the eyes of someone refusing to be drawn all the way back from whatever was engrossing her.

"Just a question . . ." I said.

"I'll come," Padma said to me. He turned to Amanda. "You go on."

She went back to her contemplation of the screen without a word. Padma got up and came to me, step-

ping into the outside room and shutting the door behind him.

"I'm trying to find Ian."

"I don't know where he'd be just now," said
Padma. "Around Gebel Nahar somewhere—but saying that's not much help.'

"Not at the size of this establishment," I nodded
toward the door he had just shut.

"It's getting rather late, isn't it," I asked, "for
Amanda to hope to turn up some sort of legal solution?"

"Not necessarily." The outer office we were standing in had its own window wall, and next to that
window wall were several of the heavily overstuffed
armchairs that were a common article of furniture in
the place. "Why don't we sit down there? If he
comes in from the corridor, he's got to go through
this office, and if he comes out on the terrace of this
level, we can see him through the window."

We went over and took chairs.

"It's not exact, actually, to say that there's a legal
way of handling this situation that Amanda's looking
for. I thought you understood that?"

"Her work is something I don't know a thing
about," I told him. "It's a specialty that grew up as
we got more and more aware that the people we
were making contracts with might have different
meanings for the same words, and different notions
of implied obligations, than we had. So we've developed people like Amanda, who steep themselves in
the differences of attitude and idea we might run
into, in the splinter cultures we deal with."

"I know," he said.

"Yes, of course you would, wouldn't you?"

"Not inevitably," he said. "It happens that as an Outbond, I wrestle with pretty much the same sort of problems that Amanda does. My work is with people who aren't Exotics, and my responsibility most of the time is to make sure we understand them—and they us. That's why I say what we have here goes far beyond legal matters."

"For example?" I found myself suddenly curious.

"You might get a better word picture if you said what Amanda is searching for is a *social* solution to the situation."

"I see," I said. "This morning Ian talked about Amanda saying that there always was a solution, but the problem here was to find it in so short a time. Did I hear that correctly—that there's always a solution to a tangle like this?"

"There's always any number of solutions," Padma said. "The problem is to find the one you'd prefer—or maybe just the one you'd accept. Human situations, being human-made, are always mutable at human hands, if you can get to them with the proper pressures before they happen. Once they happen, of course, they become history—"

He smiled at me.

"—And history, so far at least, is something we aren't able to change. But changing what's about to happen simply requires getting to the base of the forces involved in time, with the right sort of pressures exerted in the right directions. What takes time is identifying the forces, finding what pressures are possible and where to apply them."

"And we don't have time."

His smile went.

"No. In fact, you don't."

I looked squarely at him.

"In that case, shouldn't you be thinking of leaving, yourself?" I said. "According to what I gather about these Naharese, once they overrun this place, they're liable to kill anyone they come across here. Aren't you too valuable to Mara to get your throat cut by some battle-drunk soldier?"

"I'd like to think so," he said. "But you see, from our point of view, what's happening here has importances that go entirely beyond the local, or even the planetary situation. Ontogenetics identifies certain individuals as possibly being particularly influential on the history of their time. Ontogenetics, of course, can be wrong—it's been wrong before this. But we think the value of studying such people as closely as possible at certain times is important enough to take priority over everything else."

"Historically influential? Do you mean William?" I said. "Who else—not the Conde? Someone in the revolutionary camp?"

Padma shook his head.

"If we tagged certain individuals publicly as being influential men and women of their historic time, we would only prejudice their actions and the actions of the people who knew them and muddle our own conclusions about them—even if we could be sure that ontogenetics had read their importance rightly; and we can't be sure."

"You don't get out of it that easily," I said. "The fact you're physically here probably means that the individuals you're watching are right here in Gebel Nahar. I can't believe it's the Conde. His day is over, no matter how things go. That leaves the rest of us. Michael's a possibility, but he's deliberately chosen to bury himself. I know I'm not someone to shape history. Amanda? Kensie and Ian?"

He looked at me a little sadly.

"All of you, one way or another, have a hand in shaping history. But who shapes it largely, and who only a little is something I can't tell you. As I say, ontogenetics isn't that sure. As to whom I may be watching, I watch everyone."

It was a gentle, but impenetrable, shield he opposed me with. I let the matter go. I glanced out the window, but there was no sign of Ian.

"Maybe you can explain how Amanda, or you go about looking for a solution," I said.

"As I said, it's a matter of looking for the base of the existing forces at work—"

"The ranchers—and William?"

He nodded.

"Particularly William—since he's the prime mover. To get the results he wants, William or anyone else has to set up a structure of cause and effect, operating through individuals. So, for anyone else to control the forces already set to work, and bend them to different results, it's necessary to find where William's structure is vulnerable to cross-pressures and arrange for those to operate—again through individuals."

"And Amanda hasn't found a weak point yet?"

"Of course she has. Several." He frowned at me, but with a touch of humor. "I don't have any objection to telling you all this. You don't need to draw me with leading questions."

"Sorry," I said.

"It's all right. As I say, she's already found several. But none that can be implemented between now and sometime tomorrow, if the regiments attack Gebel Nahar then."

I had a strange sensation. As if a gate was slowly but inexorably being closed in my face.

"It seems to me," I said, "the easiest thing to change would be the position of the Conde. If he'd just agree to come to terms with the regiments, the whole thing would collapse."

"Obvious solutions are usually not the easiest," Padma said. "Stop and think. Why do you suppose the Conde would never change his mind?"

"He's a Naharese," I said. "More than that, he's honestly an hispanic. *El honor* forbids that he yield an inch to soldiers who were supposedly loyal to him and now are threatening to destroy him and everything he stands for."

"But tell me,' said Padma, watching me. "Even if *el honor* was satisfied, would he want to treat with the rebels?"

I shook my head.

"No," I said. It was something I had recognized before this, but only with the back of my head. As I spoke to Padma now, it was like something emerging from the shadows to stand in the full light of day. "This is the great moment of his life. This is the chance for him to substantiate that paper title of his, to make it real. This way he can prove to himself he is a real aristocrat. He'd give his life—in fact, he can hardly wait to give his life—to win that."

There was a little silence.

"So you see," said Padma. "Go on, then. What other ways do you see a solution being found?"

"Ian and Kensie could void the contract and make the penalty payment. But they won't. Aside from the fact that no responsible officer from our world would risk giving the Dorsai the sort of bad name that could give, under these special circumstances, neither of those two brothers would abandon the Conde as long as he insisted on fighting. It's as impossible for a Dorsai to do that as it is for the Conde to play games with *el honor*. Like him, their whole life has been oriented against any such thing."

"What other ways?"

"I can't think of any," I said. "I'm out of suggestions—which is probably why I was never considered for anything like Amanda's job, in the first place."

"As a matter of fact, there are a number of other possible solutions," Padma said. His voice was soft, almost pedantic. "There's the possibility of bringing counter economic pressure upon William—but there's no time for that. There's also the possibility of bringing social and economic pressure upon the ranchers; and there's the possibility of disrupting the control of the revolutionaries who've come in from outside Nahar to run this rebellion. In each case, none of these solutions are of the kind that can very easily be made to work in the short time we've got."

"In fact, there isn't any such thing as a solution that can be made to work in time, isn't that right?" I said, bluntly.

He shook his head.

"No. Absolutely wrong. If we could stop the clock at this second and take the equivalent of some months to study the situation, we'd undoubtedly find not only one, but several solutions that would abort the attack of the regiments in the time we've got to work with. What you lack isn't time in which to act, since that's merely something specified for the solution. What you lack is time in which to discover the solution that will work in the time there is to act."

"So you mean," I said, "that we're to sit here tomorrow with Michael's forty or so bandsmen—and face the attack of something like six thousand line troops, even though they're only Naharese line troops, all the time knowing that there is absolutely a way in which that attack doesn't have to happen, if only we had the sense to find it?"

"The sense—and the time," said Padma. "But yes, you're right. It's a harsh reality of life, but the sort of reality that history has turned on, since history began."

"I see," I said. "Well I find I don't accept it that easily."

"No." Padma's gaze was level and cooling upon me. "Neither does Amanda. Neither does Ian or

Kensie. Nor, I suspect, even Michael. But then, you're all Dorsai."

I said nothing. It is a little embarrassing when someone plays your own top card against you.

"In any case," Padma went on, "none of you are being called on to merely accept it. Amanda's still at work. So is Ian, so are all the rest of you. Forgive me, I didn't mean to sneer at the reflexes of your culture. I envy you—a great many people envy you—that inability to give in. My point is that the fact that we know there's an answer makes no difference. You'd all be doing the same thing anyway, wouldn't you?"

"True enough," I said—and at that moment we were interrupted.

"Padma?" It was the general office annunciator speaking from the walls around us, with Amanda's voice. "Could you give me some help, please?"

Padma got to his feet.

"I've got to go," he said.

He went out. I sat where I was, held by that odd little melancholy that had caught me up—and I think does the same with most Dorsai away from home—at moments all through my life. It is not a serious thing, just a touch of loneliness and sadness and the facing of the fact that life is measured; and there are only so many things that can be accomplished in it, try how you may.

I was still in this mood when Ian's return to the office suite by the corridor door woke me out of it.

I got up.

"Corunna!" he said, and led the way into his private office. "How's the training going?"

"As you'd expect," I said. "I left Michael alone with them, at his suggestion. He thinks they might learn faster without my presence to distract them."

"Possible," said Ian.

He stepped to the window wall and looked out. My height was not enough to let me look over the edge of the parapet on this terrace and see down to the first where the bandsmen were drilling; but I guessed that his was.

"They don't seem to be doing badly," he said.

He was still on his feet, of course, and I was standing next to his desk. I looked at it now, and found the cube holding the image Amanda had talked about. The woman pictured there was obviously not Dorsai, but there was something not unlike our people about her. She was strong-boned and dark-haired, the hair sweeping down to her shoulders, longer than most Dorsais out in the field would have worn it, but not long according to the styles of Earth.

I looked back at Ian. He had turned away from the window and his contemplation of the drill going on two levels below. But he had stopped, part way in his backturn, and his face was turned toward the wall beyond which Amanda would be working with Padma at this moment. I saw him in three-quarter's face, with the light from the window wall striking that quarter of his features that was averted from me; and I noticed a tiredness about him. Not that it showed anywhere specifically in the lines of his face. He was, as always, like a mountain of granite, untouchable. But something about the way he stood spoke of a fatigue—perhaps a fatigue of the spirit rather than of the body.

"I just heard about Leah, here," I said, nodding at the image cube, speaking to bring him back to the moment.

He turned as if his thoughts had been a long way away.

"Leah? Oh, yes." His own eyes went absently to the cube and away again. "Yes, she's Earth. I'll be going to get her after this is over. We'll be married in two months."

"That soon?" I said. "I hadn't even heard you'd fallen in love."

"Love?" he said. His eyes were still on me, but their attention had gone away again. He spoke more as if to himself than to me. "No, it was years ago I fell in love . . ."

His attention focused, suddenly. He was back with me.

"Sit down," he said, dropping into the chair behind his desk. I sat. "Have you talked to Kensie since breakfast?"

"Just a little while ago, when I was asking around to find you," I said.

"He's got a couple of runs outside the walls he'd like your hand with, tonight after dark's well settled in."

"I know," I said. "He told me about them. A sweep of the slope in front of this place to clear it before laying mines there, and a scout of the regimental camp for whatever we can learn about them before tomorrow."

■ *Gordon R. Dickson*

"That's right," Ian said.

"Do you have any solid figures on how many there are out there?"

"Regimental rolls," said Ian, "give us a total of a little over five thousand of all ranks. Fifty-two hundred and some. But something like this invariably attracts a number of Naharese who scent personal glory, or at least the chance of personal glory. Then there're perhaps seven or eight hundred honest revolutionaries in Nahar, Padma estimates, individuals who've been working to loosen the grip of the rancher oligarchy for some time. Plus a hundred or so agents provocateurs from outside."

"In something like this, those who aren't trained soldiers we can probably discount, don't you think?"

Ian nodded.

"How many of the actual soldiers'll have had any actual combat experience?" I asked.

"Combat experience in this part of Ceta," Ian said, "means having been involved in a border clash or two with the armed forces of the surrounding principalities. Maybe one in ten of the line soldiers has had that. On the other hand, every male, particularly in Nahar, has dreamed of a dramatic moment like this."

"So they'll all come on hard with the first attack," I said.

"That's as I see it," said Ian, "and Kensie agrees. I'm glad to hear it's your thought, too. Everyone out there will attack in that first charge, not merely determined to do well, but dreaming of outdoing everyone else around him. If we can throw them back even once, some of them won't come again. And that's the way it ought to go. They won't lose heart as a group. Just each setback will take the heart out of some, and we'll work them down to the hard core that's serious about being willing to die if only they can get over the walls and reach us."

"Yes," I said, "and how many of those do you think there are?"

"That's the problem," said Ian, calmly. "At the very least, there's going to be one in fifty we'll have to kill to stop. Even if half of them are already out by the time we get down to it, that's sixty of them left; and we've got to figure by that time we'll have taken at least thirty percent casualties ourselves—and that's an optimistic figure, considering the fact that these bandsmen are next thing to noncombatants. Man to man, on the kind of hardcore attackers that are going to be making it over the walls, the bandsmen that're left will be lucky to take care of an equal number of attackers. Padma, of course, doesn't exist in our defensive table of personnel. That leaves you, me, Kensie, Michael, and Amanda to handle about thirty bodies. Have you been keeping yourself in condition?"

I grinned.

"That's good," said Ian. "I forgot to figure that scar-face of yours. Be sure to smile like that when they come at you. It ought to slow them down for a couple of seconds at least, and we'll need all the help we can get."

I laughed.

"If Michael doesn't want you, how about working with Kensie for the rest of the afternoon?"

"Fine," I said.

I got up and went out. Kensie looked up from his printouts when he saw me again.

"Find him?" he asked.

"Yes. He suggested you could use me."

"I can. Join me."

We worked together the rest of the afternoon. The so-called large scale terrain maps the Naharese army library provided were hardly more useful than tourist brochures from our point of view. What Kensie needed to know was what the ground was like meter by meter from the front walls on out over perhaps a couple of hundred meters of plain beyond where the slope of the mountain met it. Given that knowledge, it would be possible to make reasonable estimates as to how a foot attack might develop, how many attackers we might be likely to have on a front, and on which parts of that front, because of vegetation, or the footing or the terrain, attackers might be expected to fall behind their fellows during a rush.

The Naharese terrain maps had never been made with such a detailed information of the ground in mind. To correct them, Kensie had spent most of the day before taking telescopic pictures of three-meter square segments of the ground, using the watch cameras built into the ramparts of the first wall. With these pictures as reference, we now proceeded to make notes on blown-up versions of the clumsy Naharese maps.

It took us the rest of the afternoon; but by the time we were finished, we had a fairly good working knowledge of the ground before the Gebel Nahar, from the viewpoint not only of someone storming up it, but from the viewpoint of a defender who might have to cover it on his belly—as Kensie and I would be doing that night. We knocked off, with the job done, finally, about the dinner hour.

In spite of having finished at a reasonable time, we found no one else at dinner but Ian. Michael was still up to his ears in the effort of teaching his bandsmen to be fighting troops; and Amanda was still with Padma, hard at the search for a solution, even at this eleventh hour.

"You'd both probably better get an hour of sleep, if you can spare the time," Ian said to me. "We might be able to pick up an hour or two more of rest just before dawn, but there's no counting on it."

"Yes," said Kensie. "And you might grab some sleep, yourself."

Brother looked at brother. They knew each other so well, they were so complete in their understanding of each other, that neither one bothered to discuss the matter further. It had been discussed silently in that one momentary exchange of glances, and now they were concerned with other things.

As it turned out, I was able to get a full three hours of sleep. It was just after ten o'clock, local time when Kensie and I came out from Gebel Nahar. On the reasonable assumption that the regiments would have watchers keeping an eye on our walls— that same watch Kensie and I were to silence so that the bandsmen could mine the slope—I had guessed we would be doing something like going out over a dark portion of the front wall on a rope. Instead, Michael was to lead us, properly outfitted and with our face and hands blackened, through some cellarways and along a passage that would let us out into the night a good fifty meters beyond the wall.

"How did you know about this?" I asked, as he took us along the passage. "If there's more secret ways like this, and the regiments know about them—"

"There aren't and they don't," said Michael. We were going almost single file down the concrete-walled tunnel as he answered me. "This is a private escape hatch that's the secret of the Conde, and no one else. His father had it built thirty-eight local years ago. Our Conde called me in to tell me about it when he heard the regiments had deserted."

I nodded. There was plainly a sympathy and a friendship between Michael and the old Conde that I had not had time to ask about. Perhaps it had come of their each being the only one of their kind in Gebel Nahar.

We reached the end of the tunnel and the foot of a short wooden ladder leading up to a circular metal hatch. Michael turned out the light in the tunnel and we were suddenly in absolute darkness. I heard him cranking something well-oiled, for it turned almost noiselessly. Above us the circular hatch lifted slowly to show starlit sky.

"Go ahead," Michael whispered. "Keep your heads down. The bushes that hide this spot have thorns at the end of their leaves."

We went up; I led, as being the more expendable of the two of us. The thorns did not stab me, although I heard them scratch against the stiff fabric of the black combat overalls I was wearing, as I pushed my way through the bushes, keeping level to the ground. I heard Kensie come up behind me and the faint sound of the hatch being closed behind us. Michael was due to open it again in two hours and fourteen minutes.

Kensie touched my shoulder. I looked and saw his hand held up, to silhouette itself against the stars. He made the hand signal for *move out*, touched me again lightly on the shoulder and disappeared. I turned away and began to move off in the opposite direction, staying close to the ground.

I had forgotten what a sweep like this was like. As with all our people, I had been raised with the idea of being always in effective physical condition. Of course, in itself, this is almost a universal idea nowadays. Most cultures emphasize keeping the physical vehicle in shape so as to be able to deliver the mental skills wherever the market may require them. But, because in our case the conditions of our work are so physically demanding, we have probably placed more emphasis on it. It has become an idea which begins in the cradle and becomes almost an ingrained reflex, like washing or brushing teeth.

This may be one of the reasons we have so many people living to advanced old age; apart from those naturally young for their years like the individuals in Amanda's family. Certainly, I think, it is one of the reasons why we tend to be active into extreme old age, right up to the moment of death. But, with the best efforts possible, even our training does not produce the same results as practice.

Ian had been right to needle me about my condition, gently as he had done it. The best facilities aboard the biggest space warships do not compare to the reality of being out in the field. My choice of work lies between the stars, but there is no denying that those like myself who spend the working years in ships grow rusty in the area of ordinary body skills. Now, at night, out next to the earth on my own, I could feel a sort of self-consciousness of my body. I was too aware of the weight of my flesh and bones, the effort my muscles made, and the awkwardness of the creeping and crawling positions in which I had to cover the ground.

I worked to the right as Kensie was working left, covering the slope segment by segment, clicking off these chunks of Cetan surface in my mind according to the memory pattern in which I had fixed them. It was all sand and gravel and low brush, most with built-in defenses in the form of thorns or burrs. The night wind blew like an invisible current around me in the darkness, cooling me under a sky where no clouds hid the stars.

The light of a moon would have been welcome, but Ceta has none. After about fifteen minutes I came to the first of nine positions that we had marked in my area as possible locations for watchers from the enemy camp. Picking such positions is a matter of simple reasoning. Anyone but the best trained of observers, given the job of watching something like the Gebel Nahar, from which no action is really expected to develop, would find the hours long. Particularly, when the hours in question are cool nighttime hours out in the middle of a plain where there is little to occupy the attention. Under those conditions, the watcher's certainty that he is simply putting in time grows steadily; and with the animal instinct in him he drifts automatically to the most comfortable or sheltered location from which to do his watching.

But there was no one at the first of the positions I came to. I moved on.

It was just about this time that I began to be aware of a change in the way I was feeling. The exercise, the adjustment of my body to the darkness and the night temperature, had begun to have their effects. I was no longer physically self-conscious. Instead, I was beginning to enjoy the action.

Old habits and reflexes had awakened in me. I flowed over the ground, now, not an intruder in the night of Nahar, but part of it. My eyes had adjusted to the dim illumination of the starlight, and I had the illusion that I was seeing almost as well as I might have in the day.

Just so, with my hearing. What had been a confusion of dark sounds had separated and identified itself as a multitude of different auditory messages. I heard the wind in the bushes without confusing it with the distant noise-making of some small, wild plains animal. I smelled the different and separate odors of the vegetation. Now I was able to hold the small sounds of my own passage—the scuff of my hands and body upon the ground—separate from the other noises that rode the steady stream of the breeze. In the end, I was not only aware of them all, I was aware of being one with them—one of the denizens of the Cetan night.

There was an excitement to it, a feeling of naturalness and rightness in my quiet search through this dim-lit land. I felt not only at home here, but as if in some measure I owned the night. The wind, the scents, the sounds I heard, all entered into me; and I recognized suddenly that I had moved completely beyond an awareness of myself as a physical body separate from what surrounded me. I was pure observer, with the keen involvement that a wild animal feels in the world he moves through. I was disembodied; a pair of eyes, a nose and two ears, sweeping invisibly through the world. I had forgotten Gebel Nahar. I had almost forgotten to think like a human. Almost—for a few moments—I had forgotten Else.

Then a sense of duty came and hauled me back to my obligations. I finished my sweep. There were no observers at all, either at any of the likely positions Kensie and I had picked out or anywhere else in the area I had covered. Unbelievable as it seemed from a military standpoint, the regiments had not even bothered to keep a token watch on us. For a second I wondered if they had never had any intention at all of attacking, as Ian had believed they would; and as everyone else, including the Conde and Michael's bandsmen, had taken for granted.

I returned to the location of the the tunnel-end, and met Kensie there. His hand-signal showed that he had also found his area deserted. There was no rea-

son why Michael's men should not be moved out as
soon as possible and put to work laying the mines.

Michael opened the hatch at the scheduled time
and we went down the ladder by feel in the darkness.
With the hatch once more closed overhead, the light
came on again.

"What did you find?" Michael asked, as we stood
squinting in the glare.

"Nothing," said Kensie. "It seems they're ignoring
us. You've got the mines ready to go?"

"Yes," said Michael. "If it's safe out there, do you
want to send the men out by one of the regular
gates? I promised the Conde to keep the secret of
this tunnel."

"Absolutely," said Kensie. "In any case, the less
people who know about this sort of way in and out
of a place like Gebel Nahar, the better. Let's go back
inside and get things organized."

We went. Back in Kensie's office, we were joined
by Amanda, who had temporarily put aside her
search for a social solution to the situation. We sat
around in a circle and Kensie and I reported on what
we had found.

"The thought occurred to me," I said, "that something might have come up to change the mind of the
Naharese about attacking here."

Kensie and Ian shook their heads so unanimously
and immediately it was as if they had reacted by instinct. The small hope in the back of my mind flickered and died. Experienced as the two of them were,
if they were that certain, there was little room for
doubt.

"I haven't waked the men yet," said Michael, "because after that drill on the weapons today they needed all the sleep they could get. I'll call the orderly and tell him to wake them now. We can be outside and at work in half an hour; and except for my rotating them in by groups for food and rest breaks, we can work straight through the night. We ought to have all the mines placed by a little before dawn."

"Good," said Ian.

I sat watching him, and the others. My sensations, outside of having become one with the night, had left my senses keyed to an abnormally sharp pitch. I was feeling now like a wild animal brought into the artificial world of indoors. The lights overhead in the office seemed harshly bright. The air itself was full of alien, mechanical scents, little trace odors carried on the ventilating system of oil and room dust, plus all the human smells that result when our race is cooped up within a structure.

And part of this sensitivity was directed toward the other four people in the room. It seemed to me that I saw, heard and smelled them with an almost painful acuity. I read the way each of them was feeling to a degree I had never been able to, before.

They were all deadly tired—each in his or her own way, very tired, with a personal, inner exhaustion that had finally been exposed by the physical tiredness to which the present situation had brought all of them except me. It seemed what that physical tiredness had accomplished had been to strip away the polite covering that before had hidden the private exhaustion; and it was now plain on every one of them.

". . . Then there's no reason for the rest of us to waste any more time," Ian was saying. "Amanda, you and I'd better dress and equip for that scout of their camp. Knife and sidearm, only."

His words brought me suddenly out of my separate awareness.

"You and Amanda?" I said. "I thought it was Kensie and I, Michael and Amanda who were going to take a look at the camp?"

"It was," said Ian. "One of the Governors who came in to talk to us yesterday is on his way in by personal aircraft. He wants to talk to Kensie again, privately—he won't talk to anyone else."

"Some kind of a deal in the offing?"

"Possibly," said Kensie. "We can't count on it, though, so we go ahead. On the other hand we can't ignore the chance. So I'll stay and Ian will go."

"We could do it with three," I said.

"Not as well as it could be done by four," said Ian. "That's a good-sized camp to get into and look over in a hurry. If anyone but Dorsai could be trusted to get in and out without being seen, I'd be glad to take half a dozen more. It's not like most military camps, where there's a single overall headquarters area. We're going to have to check the headquarters of each regiment; and there're six of them."

I nodded.

"You'd better get something to eat, Corunna," Ian went on. "We could be out until dawn."

It was good advice. When I came back from eating, the other three who were to go were already in Ian's office, and outfitted. On his right thigh Michael was wearing a knife—which was after all, more tool than weapon—but he wore no sidearms and I noticed Ian did not object. With her hands and face blacked, wearing the black stocking cap, overalls and boots, Amanda looked taller and more square-shouldered than she had in her daily clothes.

"All right," said Ian. He had the plan of the camp laid out, according to our telescopic observation of it through the rampart watch-cameras, combined with what Michael had been able to tell us of Naharese habits.

"We'll go by field experience," he said. "I'll take two of the six regiments—the two in the center. Michael, because he's more recently from his Academy training and because he knows these people, will take two regiments—the two on the left wing that includes the far left one that was his own Third Regiment. You'll take the Second Regiment, Corunna, and Amanda will take the Fourth. I mention this now in case we don't have a chance to talk outside the camp."

"It's unlucky you and Michael can't take regiments adjoining each other," I said. "That'd give you a chance to work together. You might need that with two regiments apiece to cover."

"Ian needs to see the Fifth Regiment for himself, if possible," Michael said. "That's the Guard Regiment, the one with the best arms. And since my regiment is a traditional enemy of the Guard Regiment, the two have deliberately been separated as far as possible—that's why the Guards are in the middle and my Third's on the wing."

"Anything else? Then we should go," said Ian.

We went out quietly by the same tunnel by which Kensie and I had gone for our sweep of the slope, leaving the hatch propped a little open against our return. Once in the open we spread apart at about a ten meter interval and began to jog toward the lights of the regimental camp, in the distance.

We were a little over an hour coming up on it. We began to hear it when we were still some distance from it. It did not resemble a military camp on the eve of battle half so much as it did a large open-air party.

The camp was laid out in a crescent. The center of each regimental area was made up of the usual beehive-shaped buildings of blown bubble-plastic that could be erected so easily on the spot. Behind and between the clumpings of these were ordinary tents of all types and sizes. There was noise and steady traffic between these tents and the plastic buildings as well as between the plastic buildings themselves.

We stopped a hundred meters out, opposite the center of the crescent and checked off. We were able to stand talking, quite openly. Even if we had been without our black accoutrements, the general sound and activity going on just before us ensured as much privacy and protection as a wall between us and the camp would have afforded.

"All back here in forty minutes," Ian said.

We checked chronometers and split up, going in. My target, the Second Regiment, was between Ian's two regiments and Michael's two; and it was a section that had few tents, these seeming to cluster most thickly either toward the center of the camp or out on both wings. I slipped between the first line of buildings, moving from shadow to shadow. It was foolishly easy. Even if I had not already loosened myself up on the scout across the slope before Gebel Nahar, I would have found it easy. It was very clear that even if I had come, not in scouting blacks but wearing ordinary local clothing and obviously mispronouncing the local Spanish accent, I could have strolled freely and openly wherever I wanted. Individuals in all sorts of civilian clothing were intermingled with the uniformed military; and it became plain almost immediately that few of the civilians were known by name and face to the soldiers. Ironically, my night battle dress was the one outfit that would have attracted unwelcome attention—if they had noticed me.

But there was no danger that they would notice me. Effectively, the people moving between the buildings and among the tents had neither eyes nor ears for what was not directly under their noses. Getting about unseen under such conditions boils down simply to the fact that you move quietly—which means moving all of you in a single rhythm, including your breathing; and that when you stop, you become utterly still—which means being completely relaxed in whatever bodily position you have stopped in.

Breathing is the key to both, of course, as we learn back home in childhood games even before we are school age. Move in rhythm and stop utterly and you

can sometimes stand in plain sight of someone who
does not expect you to be there, and go unobserved.
How many times has everyone had the experience of
being looked "right through" by someone who does
not expect to see them at a particular place or moment?

So, there was no difficulty in what I had to do; and
as I say, my experience on the slope had already
keyed me. I fell back into my earlier feeling of being
nothing but senses—eyes, ears, and nose, drifting invisibly through the scenes of the Naharese camp. A
quick circuit of my area told me all we needed to
know about this particular regiment.

Most of the soldiers were between late twenties
and early forties in age. Under other conditions this
might have meant a force of veterans. In this case, it
indicated just the opposite, time-servers who liked
the uniform, the relatively easy work, and the authority and freedom of being in the military. I found a
few field energy weapons—light, three-man pieces
that were not only out-of-date, but impractical to
bring into action in open territory like that before
Gebel Nahar. The heavier weapons we had emplaced
on the ramparts would be able to take out such as
these almost as soon as the rebels could try to put
them into action, and long before they could do any
real damage to the heavy defensive walls.

The hand weapons varied, ranging from the best of
newer energy guns, cone rifles and needle guns—in
the hands of the soldiers—to the strangest assortment
of ancient and modern hunting tools and slug-
throwing sport pieces—carried by those in civilian

clothing. I did not see any crossbows or swords; but it would not have surprised me if I had. The civilian and the military hand weapons alike, however, had one thing in common that surprised me, in the light of everything else I saw—they were clean, well-cared for, and handled with respect.

I decided I had found out as much as necessary about this part of the camp. I headed back to the first row of plastic structures and the darkness of the plains beyond, having to detour slightly to avoid a drunken brawl that had spilled out of one of the buildings into the space between it and the next. In fact, there seemed to be a good deal of drinking and drugging going on, although none of those I saw had got themselves to the edge of unconsciousness yet.

It was on this detour that I became conscious of someone quietly moving parallel to me. In this place and time, it was highly unlikely that there was any-one who could do so with any secrecy and skill ex-cept one of us who had come out from Gebel Nahar. Since it was on the side of my segment that touched the area given to Michael to investigate, I guessed it was he. I went to look, and found him.

I've got something to show you, he hand signalled me. *Are you done, here?*

Yes, I told him.

Come on, then.

He led me into his area, to one of the larger plastic buildings in the territory of the second regiment he had been given to investigate. He brought me to the building's back. The curving sides of such structures are not difficult to climb quietly if you have had some practice doing so. He led me to the top of the roof curve and pointed at a small hole.

I looked in and saw six men with the collar tabs of Regimental Commanders, sitting together at a table, apparently having sometime since finished a meal. Also present were some officers of lesser rank, but none of these were at the table. Bubble plastic, in addition to its other virtues, is a good sound baffle; and since the table and those about it were not directly under the observation hole, but over against one of the curving walls, some distance off, I could not make out their conversation. It was just below comprehension level. I could hear their words, but not understand them.

But I could watch the way they spoke and their gestures, and tell how they were reacting to each other. It became evident, after a few minutes, that there were a great many tensions around that table. There was no open argument, but they sat and looked at each other in ways that were next to open challenges and the rumble of their voices bristled with the electricity of controlled angers.

I felt my shoulder tapped, and took my attention from the hole to the night outside. It took a few seconds to adjust to the relative darkness on top of the structure; but when I did, I could see the Michael was again talking to me with his hands.

Look at the youngest of the Commanders—the one on your left, with the very black mustache. That's the Commander of my regiment.

I looked, identified the man, and lifted my gaze from the hole briefly to nod.

Now look across the table and as far down from him as possible. You see the somewhat heavy Commander with the gray sideburns and the lips that almost pout?

I looked, raised my head and nodded again.

That's the Commander of the Guard Regiment. He and my Commander are beginning to wear on each other. If not, they'd be seated side by side and pretending that anything that ever was between their two regiments has been put aside. It's almost as bad with the junior officers, if you know the signs to look for in each one's case. Can you guess what's triggered it off?

No, I told him, *but I suppose you do, or you wouldn't have brought me here.*

I've been watching for some time. They had the maps out earlier, and it was easy to tell what they were discussing. It's the position of each regiment in the line of battle, tomorrow. They've agreed what it's to be, at last, but no one's happy with the final decision.

I nodded.

I wanted you to see it for yourself. They're all ready to go at each other's throats and it's an explosive situation. Maybe Amanda can find something in it she can use. I brought you here because I was hoping that when we go back to rendezvous with the others, you'll support me in suggesting she come and see this for herself.

I nodded again. The brittle emotions betrayed by the commanders below had been obvious, even to me, the moment I had first looked through the hole.

We slipped quietly back down the curve of the building to the shadowed ground at its back and moved out together toward the rendezvous point.

We had no trouble making our way out through the rest of the encampment and back to our meeting spot. It was safely beyond the illumination of the lights that the regiments had set up amongst their buildings. Ian and Amanda were already there; and we stood together, looking back at the activity in the encampment as we compared notes.

"I called Captain El Man in to look at something I'd found," Michael said. "In my alternate area, there was a meeting going on between the regimental commanders—"

The sound of a shot from someone's antique explosive firearm cut him short. We all turned toward the encampment; and saw a lean figure wearing a white shirt brilliantly reflective in the lights, running toward us, while a gang of men poured out of one of the tents, stared about, and then started in pursuit.

The one they chased was running directly for us, in his obvious desire to get away from the camp. It would have been easy to believe that he had seen us and was running to us for help; but the situation did not support that conclusion. Aside from the unlikeliness of his seeking aid from strangers dressed and equipped as we were, it was obvious that with his eyes still dilated from the lights of the camp, and staring at black-dressed figures like ours, he was completely unable to see us.

All of us dropped flat into the sparse grass of the

plain. But he still came straight for us. Another shot sounded from his pursuers.

It only seems, of course, that the luck in such situations is always bad. It is not so, of course. Good and bad balance out. But knowing this does not help when things seem freakishly determined to do their worst. The fugitive had all the open Naharese plain into which to run. He came toward us instead as if drawn on a cable. We lay still. Unless he actually stepped on one of us, there was a chance he could run right through us and not know we were there.

He did not step on one of us, but he did trip over Michael, stagger on a step, check, and glance down to see what had interrupted his flight. He looked directly at Amanda, and stopped, staring down in astonishment. A second later, he had started to swing around to face his pursuers, his mouth open to shout to them.

Whether he had expected the information of what he had found to soothe their anger toward him, or whether he had simply forgotten at that moment that they had been chasing him, was beside the point. He was obviously about to betray our presence, and Amanda did exactly the correct thing—even if it produced the least desirable results. She uncoiled from the ground like a spring released from tension, one fist taking the fugitive in the Adam's apple to cut off his cry and the other going into him just under the breastbone to take the wind out of him and put him down without killing him.

She had been forced to rise between him and his pursuers. But, all black as she was in contrast to the brilliant whiteness of his shirt, she would well have flickered for a second before their eyes without being recognized; and with the man down, we could have slipped away from the pursuers without their realizing until too late that we had been there. But the incredible bad luck of that moment was still with us.

As she took the man down, another shot sounded from the pursuers, clearly aimed at the now-stationary target of the fugitive—and Amanda went down with him.

She was up again in a second.

"Fine—I'm fine," she said. "Let's go!"

We went, fading off into the darkness at the same steady trot at which we had come to the camp. Until we were aware of specific pursuit there was no point in burning up our reserves of energy. We moved steadily away, back toward Gebel Nahar, while the pursuers finally reached the fugitive, surrounded him, got him on his feet and talking.

By that time we could see them flashing around them the lights some of them had been carrying, searching the plain for us. But we were well away by that time, and drawing farther off every second. No pursuit developed.

"Too bad," said Ian, as the sound and lights of the camp dwindled behind us. "But no great harm done. What happened to you, 'Manda?"

She did not answer. Instead, she went down again, stumbling and dropping abruptly. In a second we were all back and squatting around her.

She was plainly having trouble breathing.

"Sorry . . ." she whispered.

Ian was already cutting away the clothing over her left shoulder.

"Not much blood," he said.

The tone of his voice said he was very angry with her. So was I. It was entirely possible that she might have killed herself by trying to run with a wound that should not have been excited by that kind of treatment. She had acted instinctively to hide the knowledge that she had been hit by that last shot, so that the rest of us would not hesitate in getting away safely. It was not hard to understand the impulse that had made her do it—but she should not have.

"Corunna," said Ian, moving aside. "This is more in your line."

He was right. As a captain, I was the closest thing to a physician aboard, most of the time. I moved in beside her and checked the wound as best I could. In the general but faint starlight it showed as merely a small patch of darkness against a larger, pale patch of exposed flesh. I felt it with my fingers and put my cheek down against it.

"Small caliber slug," I said. Ian breathed a little harshly out through his nostrils. He had already deduced that much. I went on. "Not a sucking wound. High up, just below the collarbone. No immediate pneumothorax, but the chest cavity'll be filling with blood. Are you very short of breath, Amanda? Don't talk, just nod or shake your head."

She nodded.

"How do you feel. Dizzy? Faint?"

She nodded again. Her skin was clammy to my touch.

"Going into shock," I said.

I put my ear to her chest again.

"Right," I said. "The lung on this side's not filling with air. She can't run. She shouldn't do anything. We'll need to carry her."

"I'll do that," said Ian. He was still angry— irrationally, emotionally angry, but trying to control it. "How fast do we have to get her back, do you think?"

"Her condition ought to stay the same for a couple of hours," I said. "Looks like no large blood vessels were hit; and the smaller vessels tend to be self-sealing. But the pleural cavity on this side has been filling up with blood and she's collapsed a lung. That's why she's having trouble breathing. No blood around her mouth, so it probably didn't nick an air-way going through . . ."

I felt around behind her shoulder but found no exit wound.

"It didn't go through. If there're MASH med-mech units back at Gebel Nahar and we get her back in the next two hours, she should be all right—if we carry her."

Ian scooped her into his arms. He stood up.

"Head down," I said.

"Right," he answered and put her over one shoulder in a fireman's carry. "No, wait—we'll need some padding for my shoulder."

Michael and I took off our jerseys and made a pad for his other shoulder. He transferred her to that shoulder, with her head hanging down his back. I sympathized with her. Even with the padding, it was not a comfortable way to travel; and her wound and shortness of breath would make it a great deal worse.

"Try it at a slow walk, first," I said.

"I'll try it. But we can't go slow walk all the way," said Ian. "It's nearly three klicks from where we are now."

He was right, of course. To walk her back over a distance of three kilometers would take too long. I went behind him to watch her as well as could be done. The sooner I got her to a med-mech unit the better. We started off, and he gradually increased his pace until we were moving smoothly but briskly.

"How are you?" he asked her, over his shoulder.

"She nodded," I reported, from my position behind him.

"Good," he said, and began to jog.

We travelled. She made no effort to speak, and none of the rest of us spoke. From time to time I moved up closer behind Ian to watch her at close range; and as far as I could tell, she did not lose consciousness once on that long, jolting ride; Ian forged ahead, something made of steel rather than of ordinary human flesh, his gaze fixed on the lights of Gebel Nahar, far off across the plain.

There is something that happens under those conditions where the choice is either to count the seconds, or disregard time altogether. In the end we all—and I think Amanda, too, as far as she was capable of controlling how she felt—went off a little way from ordinary time, and did not come back to it until we were at the entrance to the Conde's secret tunnel, leading back under the walls of Gebel Nahar.

By the time I got Amanda laid out in the medical section of Gebel Nahar, she looked very bad indeed and was only semi-conscious. Anything else, of course, would have been surprising indeed. It does not improve the looks of even a very healthy person to be carried head down for over thirty minutes. Luckily, the medical section had everything necessary in the way of med-mechs. I was able to find a portable unit that could be rigged for bed rest— vacuum pump, power unit, drainage bag. It was a matter of inserting a tube between Amanda's lung and chest wall—and this I left to the med-mech, which was less liable to human mistakes than I was on a day in which luck seemed to be running so badly—so that the unit could exhaust the blood from the pleural space into which it had drained.

It was also necessary to rig a unit to supply her with reconstituted whole blood while this draining process was going on. However, none of this was difficult, even for a part-trained person like myself, once we got her safely to the medical section. I finally got her fixed up and left her to rest—she was in no shape to do much else.

I went off to the offices to find Ian and Kensie. They were both there; and they listened without interrupting to my report on Amanda's treatment and my estimate of her condition.

"She should rest for the next few days, I take it," said Ian when I was done.

"That's right," I said.

"There ought to be some way we could get her out

of here, to safety and a regular hospital," said Kensie.

"How?" I asked. "It's almost dawn now. The Naharese would zero in on any vehicle that tried to leave this place, by ground or air. It'd never get away."

Kensie nodded soberly.

"They should," said Ian, "be starting to move now, if this dawn was to be the attack moment."

He turned to the window, and Kensie and I turned with him. Dawn was just breaking. The sky overhead was white-blue and hard, and the brown stretch of the plain looked also stony and hard and empty between the Gebel Nahar and the distant line of the encampment. It was very obvious, even without vision amplification, that the soldiers and others in the encampment had not even begun to form up in battle positions, let alone begin to move toward us.

"After all their parties last night, they may not get going until noon," I said.

"I don't think they'll be that late," said Ian, absently. He had taken me seriously. "At any rate, it gives us a little more time. Are you going to have to stay with Amanda?"

"I'll want to look in on her from time to time—in fact, I'm going back down now," I said. "I just came up to tell you how she is. But in between visits, I can be useful."

"Good," said Ian. "As soon as you've had another look at her, why don't you go see if you can help Michael. He's been saying he's got his doubts about those bandsmen of his."

"All right," I went out.

When I got back to the medical section, Amanda was asleep. I was going to slip out and leave her to rest, when she woke and recognized me.

"Corunna," she said, "how am I?"

"You're fine," I said, going back to the side of the bed where she lay. "All you need now is to get a lot of sleep and do a good job of healing."

"What's the situation outside?" she said. "Is it day, yet?"

We were in one of the windowless rooms in the interior of Gebel Nahar.

"Just dawn," I said. "Nothing happening so far. In any case, you forget about all that and rest."

"You'll need me up there."

"Not with a tube between your ribs," I said. "Lie back and sleep."

Her head moved restlessly on the pillow.

"It might have been better if that slug had been more on target."

I looked down at her.

"According to what I've heard about you," I said, "you of all people ought to know that when you're in a hospital bed it's not the best time in the world to be worrying over things."

She started to speak, interrupted herself to cough, and was silent for a little time until the pain of the tube, rubbing inside her with the disturbance of her coughing, subsided. Even a deep breath would move that tube now, and pain her. There was nothing to be done about that, but I could see how shallowly she breathed, accordingly.

"No," she said. "I can't want to die. But the situation as it stands, is impossible; and every way out of it there is, is impossible, for all three of us. Just like our situation here in Gebel Nahar with no way out."

"Kensie and Ian are able to make up their own minds."

"It's not a matter of making up minds. It's a matter of impossibilities."

"Well," I said, "is there anything you can do about that?"

"I ought to be able to."

"Ought to, maybe, but can you?"

She breathed shallowly. Slowly she shook her head on the pillow.

"Then let it go. Leave it alone," I said. "I'll be back to check on you from time to time. Wait and see what develops."

"How can I wait?" she said. "I'm afraid of myself. Afraid I might throw everything overboard and do what I want most—and so ruin everyone."

"You won't do that."

"I might."

"You're exhausted," I told her. "You're in pain. Stop trying to think. I'll be back in an hour or two to check on you. Until then, rest!"

I went out.

I took the corridors that led me to the band section. I saw no other bandsmen in the corridors as I approached their section, but an orderly was on duty as usual in Michael's outer office and Michael himself was in his own office, standing beside his desk with a sheaf of printed records in hand.

"Captain!" he said, when he saw me.

"I've got to look in on Amanda from time to time," I said. "But in between, Ian suggested you might find me useful."

"I'd always find you useful, sir," he said, with the ghost of a smile. "Do you want to come along to stores with me? I need to check a few items of supply and we can talk as we go."

"Of course."

We left the offices and he led me down other corridors and into a supply section. What he was after, it developed, was not the supplies themselves, but the automated delivery system that would keep feeding them, on command—or at regular intervals, without command, if the communications network was knocked out—to various sections of Gebel Nahar. It was a system of a sort I had never seen before.

"Another of the ways the ranchers who designed this looked ahead to having to hole up here," Michael explained as we looked at the supply bins for each of the various sections of the fortress, each bin already stocked with the supplies it would deliver as needed. He was going from bin to bin, checking the contents of each and testing each delivery system to make sure it was working.

The overhead lights were very bright, and their illumination reflected off solid concrete walls painted a utilitarian, flat white. The effect was both blinding and bleak at once; and the feeling of bleakness was reinforced by the stillness of the air. The ventilators must have been working here as in other interior parts of the Gebel Nahar, but with the large open space of the supply section and its high ceilings, the air felt as if there was no movement to it at all.

"Lucky for us," I said.

Michael nodded.

"Yes, if ever a place was made to be defended by a handful of people, this is it. Only, they didn't expect the defense to be by such a small handful as we are. They were thinking in terms of a hundred families, with servants and retainers. Still, if it comes to a last stand for us in the inner fort, on the top three levels, they're going to have to pay one hell of a price to get at us."

I watched his face as he worked. There was no doubt about it. He looked much more tired, much leaner, and older than he had appeared to me only a few days before when he had met Amanda and me at the spaceport terminal of Nahar City. But the work he had been doing and what he had gone through could not alone have been enough to cut him down so visibly, at his age.

He finished checking the last of the delivery systems and the last of the bins. He turned away.

"Ian tells me you've got some concern as to how your bandsmen may stand up to the attack," I said.

His mouth thinned and straightened.

"Yes," he said. There was a little pause, and then he added: "You can't blame them. If they'd been real soldier types they would have been in one of the line companies. There's security, but no chance of promotion to speak of, in a band."

Then humor came back to him, a tired but real smile.

"Of course, for someone like myself," he said, "that's ideal."

"On the other hand," I said. "They're here with us. They stayed."

"Well . . ." He sat down a little heavily on a short stack of boxes and waved me to another, "so far it hasn't cost them anything but some hard work. And they've been paid off in excitement. I think I said something to you about that when we were flying out from Nahar City. Excitement—drama—is what most Naharese live for; and die for, for that matter, if the drama is big enough."

"You don't think they'll fight when the time comes?"

"I don't know." His face was bleak again. "I only know I can't blame them—I can't, of all people—if they don't."

"Your attitude's a matter of conviction."

"Maybe theirs is, too. There's no way to judge any one person by another. You never know enough to make a real comparison."

"True," I said. "But I still think that if they don't fight, it'll be for somewhat lesser reasons than yours for not fighting."

He shook his head slowly.

"Maybe I'm wrong, all wrong." His tone was almost bitter. "But I can't get outside myself to look at it. I only know I'm afraid."

"Afraid?" I looked at him. "Of fighting?"

"I wish it was of fighting," he laughed, briefly. "No, I'm afraid that I don't have the will *not* to fight. I'm afraid that at the last moment it'll all come back, all those early dreams and all the growing up and all the training—and I'll find myself killing, even though I'll know that it won't make any difference in the end and that the Naharese will take Gebel Nahar anyway."

"I don't think it'd be Gebel Nahar you'd be fighting for," I said slowly. "I think it'd be out of a natural, normal instinct to stay alive yourself as long as you can—or to help protect those who are fighting alongside you."

"Yes," he said. His nostrils flared as he drew in an unhappy breath. "The rest of you. That's what I won't be able to stand. It's too deep in me. I might be able to stand there and let myself be killed. But can I stand there when they start to kill someone else—like Amanda, and she already wounded?"

There was nothing I could say to him. But the irony of it rang in me, just the same. Both he and Amanda, afraid that their instincts would lead them to do what their thinking minds had told them they should not do. He and I walked back to his office in silence. When we arrived, there was a message that had been left with Michael's orderly, for me, to call Ian.

I did. His face looked out of the phone screen at me, as unchanged as ever.

"The Naharese still haven't started to move," he said. "They're so unprofessional I'm beginning to think that perhaps we can get Padma, at least, away from here. He can take one of the small units from the vehicle pool and fly out toward Nahar City. My guess is that once they stop him and see he's an Exotic, they'll simply wave him on."

"It could be," I said.

"I'd like you to go and put that point to him," said Ian. "He seems to want to stay, for reasons of his own, but he may listen if you make him see that by staying here, he simply increases the load of responsibility on the rest of us. I'd like to order him out of here; but he knows I don't have the authority for that."

"What makes you think I'm the one to talk him into going?"

"It'd have to be one of the senior officers here, to get him to listen," said Ian. "Both Kensie and I are too tied up to take the time. While even if either one was capable, Michael's a bad choice and Amanda's flat in bed."

"All right," I said. "I'll go talk to him right now. Where is he?"

"In his quarters, I understand. Michael can tell you how to find them."

I reached Padma's suite without trouble. In fact, it was not far from the suite of rooms that had been assigned to me. I found Padma seated at his desk making a recording. He broke off when I stepped into his sitting room in answer to his invitation, which had followed my knock on his door.

"If you're busy, I can drop back in a little while," I said.

"No, no." He swung his chair around, away from the desk. "Sit down. I'm just doing up a report for whoever comes out from the Exotics to replace me."

"You won't need to be replaced if you'll leave now," I said. It was a blunt beginning, but he had given me the opening and time was not plentiful.

"I see," he said. "Did Ian or Kensie ask you to talk to me, or is this the result of an impulse of your own?"

"Ian asked me," I said. "The Naharese are delaying their attack, and he thinks that they're so generally disorganized and unmilitary that there's a chance for you to get safely away to Nahar City. They'll undoubtedly stop whatever vehicle you'd take, when they see it coming out of Gebel Nahar. But once they see you're an Exotic—"

His smile interrupted me.

"All right," I said. "Tell me. Why shouldn't they let you pass when they see you're an Exotic? All the worlds know Exotics are noncombatants."

"Perhaps," he said. "Unfortunately, William has made a practice of identifying us as the machiavellian practitioners at the roots of whatever trouble and evil there is to be found anywhere. At the moment most of the Naharese have an image of me that's half-demon, half-enemy. In their present mood of license, most of them would probably welcome the chance to shoot me on sight."

I stared at him. He was smiling.

"If that's the case, why didn't you leave days ago?" I asked him.

"I have my duty, too. In this instance, it's to gather information for those on Mara and Kultis." His smile broadened. "Also, there's the matter of my own temperament. Watching a situation like the one here is fascinating. I wouldn't leave now if I could. In short, I'm as chained here as the rest of you, even if it is for different reasons."

I shook my head at him.

"It's a fine argument," I said. "But if you'll forgive me, it's a little hard to believe."

"In what way?"

"I'm sorry," I told him, "but I don't seem to be able to give any real faith to the idea that you're being held here by patterns that are essentially the same as mine, for instance."

"Not the same," he said. "Equivalent. The fact others can't match you Dorsai in your own particular area doesn't mean those others don't have equal areas in which equal commitments apply to them. The physics of life works in all of us. It simply manifests itself differently with different people."

"With identical results?"

"With comparable results—could I ask you to sit down?" Padma said mildly. "I'm getting a stiff neck looking up at you."

I sat down facing him.

"For example," he said. "In the Dorsai ethic, you and the others here have something that directly justifies your natural human hunger to do things for great purposes. The Naharese here have no equivalent ethic; but they feel the hunger just the same. So they invent their own customs, their *leto de muerte* concepts. But can you Dorsais, of all people, deny that their concepts can lead them to as true a heroism, or as true a keeping of faith as your ethic leads you to?"

"Of course I can't deny," I said. "But my people can at least be counted on to perform as expected. Can the Naharese?"

"No. But note the dangers of the fact that Dorsais are known to be trustworthy, Exotics known to be personally nonviolent, the church soldiers of the Friendly Worlds known to be faith-holders. That very knowledge tends too often to lead one to take for granted that trustworthiness is the exclusive property of the Dorsai, that there are no truly non-violent individuals not wearing Exotic robes, and that the faith of anyone not a Friendly must be weak and unremarkable. We are all human and struck with the whole spectrum of the human nature. For clear thinking, it's necessary to first assume that the great hungers and responses are there in everyone—then simply go look for them in all people—including the Naharese."

"You sound a little like Michael when you get on the subject of the Naharese." I got up. "All right, have it your way and stay if you want. I'm going to leave now, myself, before you talk me into going out and offering to surrender before they even get here."

He laughed. I left.

It was time again for me to check Amanda. I went to the medical section. But she was honestly asleep now. Apparently she had been able to put her personal concerns aside enough so that she could exercise a little of the basic physiological control we are all taught from birth. If she had, it could be that she would spend most of the next twenty-four hours sleeping, which would be the best thing for her. If the Naharese did not manage, before that time was up, to break through to the inner fort where the medical section was, she would have taken a large stride toward healing herself. If they did break through she would need whatever strength she could gain between now and then.

It was a shock to see the sun as high in the sky as it was, when I emerged from the blind walls of the corridors once more, on to the first terrace. The sky was almost perfectly clear and there was a small, steady breeze. The day would be hot. Ian and Kensie were each standing at one end of the terrace and looking through watch cameras at the Naharese front.

Michael, the only other person in sight, was also at a watch camera, directly in front of the door I had come out. I went to him and he looked up as I reached him.

"They're on the move," he said, stepping back from the watch camera. I looked into its rectangular viewing screen, bright with the daylight scene it showed under the shadow of the battle armor hooding the camera. He was right. The regiments had finally formed for the attack and were now moving toward us with their portable field weapons, at the pace of a slow walk across the intervening plain.

I could see their regimental and company flags spaced out along the front of the crescent formation and whipping in the morning breeze. The Guard Regiment was still in the center and Michael's Third Regiment out on the right wing. Behind the two wings I could see the darker swarms that were the volunteers and the revolutionaries, in their civilian clothing.

The attacking force had already covered a third of the distance to us. I stepped away from the screen of the camera, and all at once the front of men I looked at became a thin line with little bright flashes of reflected sunlight and touches of color all along it, still distant under the near-cloudless sky and the climbing sun.

"Another thirty or forty minutes before they reach us," said Michael.

I looked at him. The clear daylight showed him as pale and wire-tense. He looked as if he had been whittled down until nothing but nerves were left. He was not wearing weapons, although at either end of the terrace, Ian and Kensie both had sidearms clipped to their legs, and behind us there were racks of cone rifles ready for use.

The rifles woke me to something I had subconsciously noted but not focused upon. The bays with the fixed weapons were empty of human figures.

"Where're your bandsmen?" I asked Michael.

He gazed at me.

"They're gone," he said.

"Gone?"

"Decamped. Run off. Deserted, if you want to use that word."

I stared at him.

"You mean they've joined—"

"No, no." He broke in on me as if the question I was just about to ask was physically painful to him. "They haven't gone over to the enemy. They just decided to save their own skins. I told you—you remember, I told you they might. You can't blame them. They're not Dorsai; and staying here meant certain death for them."

"If Gebel Nahar is overrun," I said.

"Can you believe it won't be?"

"It's become hard to," I said, "now that there's just us. But there's always a chance as long as anyone's left to fight. At Baunpore, I saw men and women firing from hospital beds, when the North Freilanders broke in."

I should not have said it. I saw the shadow cross his eyes and knew he had taken my reference to Baunpore personally, as if I had been comparing his present weaponless state with the last efforts of the defenders I had seen then. There were times when my scars became more curse than blessing.

"That's a general observation, only," I told him. "I don't mean to accuse—"

"It's not what you accuse me of, it's what I accuse me of," he said, in a low voice looking out at the oncoming regiments. "I knew what it meant when my bandsmen took off. But I also understand how they could decide to do it."

There was nothing more I could say. We both knew that without his forty men we could not even make a pretence of holding the first terrace past the moment when the first line of Naharese would reach the base of the ramparts. There were just too few of us and too many of them to stop them from coming over the top.

"They're probably hiding just out beyond the

walls," he said. He was still talking about his former bandsmen. "If we do manage to hold out for a day or two, there's a slight chance they might trickle back—"

He broke off, staring past me. I turned and saw Amanda.

How she had managed to do it by herself, I do not know. But, clearly, she had gotten herself out of her hospital bed and strapped the portable drainage unit on to her. It was not heavy or much bigger than a thick book; and it was designed for wearing by an ambulatory patient, but it must have been hell for her to rig it by herself with that tube rubbing inside her at every deep breath.

Now she was here, looking as if she might collapse at any time, but on her feet with the unit slung from her right shoulder and strapped to her right side. She had a sidearm clipped to her left thigh, over the cloth of the hospital gown; and the gown itself had been ripped up the center so that she could walk in it.

"What the hell are you doing up here?" I snarled at her. "Get back to bed!"

"Corunna—" she gave me the most level and unyielding stare I have ever encountered from anyone in my life, "don't give me orders. I rank you."

I blinked at her. It was true I had been asked to be her driver for the trip here, and in a sense that put me under her orders. But for her to presume to tell a Captain of a full flight of fighting ships, with an edge of half a dozen years in seniority and experience that in a combat situation like this she ranked him—it was raving nonsense. I opened my mouth to explode—and found myself bursting out in laughter, instead. The situation was too ridiculous. Here we were, five people even counting Michael, facing three thousand; and I was about to let myself get trapped into an argument over who ranked who. Aside from the fact that only the accident of her present assignment gave her any claim to superiority over me, relative rank between Dorsai had always been a matter of local conditions and situations, tempered with a large pinch of common sense.

But, obviously she was out here on the terrace to stay; and obviously, I was not going to make any real issue of it under the circumstances. We both understood what was going on. Which did not change the fact that she should not have been on her feet. Like Ian out on the plain, and in spite of having been forced to see the funny side of it, I was still angry with her.

"The next time you're wounded, you better hope I'm not your medico," I told her. "What do you think you can do up here, anyway?"

"I can be with the rest of you," she said.

I closed my mouth again. There was no arguing with that answer. Out of the corner of my eyes I saw Kensie and Ian approaching from the far ends of the terrace. In a moment they were with us.

They looked down at her but said nothing, and we all turned to look again out across the plain.

The Naharese front had been approaching steadily. It was still too far away to be seen as a formation of individuals. It was still just a line of different shade

■ *Gordon R. Dickson*

than the plain itself, touched with flashes of light and
spots of color. But it was a line with a perceptible
thickness now.

We stood together, the four of us, looking at the
slow, ponderous advance upon us. All my life, as just
now with Amanda, I had been plagued by a sudden
awareness of the ridiculous. It came on me now.
What mad god had decided that an army should
march against a handful—and that the handful should
not only stand to be marched upon, but should pre-
pare to fight back? But then the sense of the ridiculousness passed. The Naharese would continue to
come on because all their lives had oriented them
against Gebel Nahar. We would oppose them when
they came because all our lives had been oriented to
fighting for even lost causes, once we had become
committed to them. In another time and place it
might be different for those of us on both sides. But
this was the here and now.

With that, I passed into the final stage that always
came on me before battle. It was as if I stepped down
into a place of private peace and quiet. What was
coming would come, and I would meet it when it
came. I was aware of Kensie, Ian, Michael and
Amanda standing around me, and aware that they
were experiencing much the same feelings. Something like a telepathy flowed between us, binding us
together in a feeling of particular unity. In my life
there has been nothing like that feeling of unity, and
I have noticed that those who have once felt it never
forget it. It is as it is, as it always has been, and we

■ 122

who are there at that moment are together. Against
that togetherness, odds no longer matter.

There was a faint scuff of a foot on the terrace
floor, and Michael was gone. I looked at the others,
and the thought was unspoken between us. He had
gone to put on his weapons. We turned once more to
the plain, and saw the approaching Naharese now
close enough so that they were recognizable as individual figures. They were almost close enough for
the sound of their approach to be heard by us.

We moved forward to the parapet of the terraces
and stood watching. The day-breeze, strengthening,
blew in our faces. There was time now to appreciate
the sunlight, the not-yet-hot temperature of the day
and the moving air. Another few hundred meters and
they would be within the range of maximum efficiency for our emplaced weapons—and we, of
course, within range of their portables. Until then,
there was nothing urgent to be done.

The door opened behind us. I turned, but it was
not Michael. It was Padma, supporting El Conde,
who was coming out to us with the help of a silver-
headed walking stick. Padma helped him out to
where we stood at the parapet, and for a second he
ignored us, looking instead out at the oncoming
troops. Then he turned to us.

"Gentlemen and lady," he said in Spanish, "I have
chosen to join you."

"We're honored," Ian answered him in the same
tongue. "Would you care to sit down?"

"Thank you, no. I will stand. You may go about
your duties."

He leaned on the cane, watching across the parapet and paying no attention to us. We stepped back away from him, and Padma spoke in a low voice.

"I'm sure he won't be in the way," Padma said. "But he wanted to be down here, and there was no one but me left to help him."

"It's all right," said Kensie. "But what about you?"

"I'd like to stay, too," said Padma.

Ian nodded. A harsh sound came from the throat of the count, and we looked at him. He was rigid as some ancient dry spearshaft, staring out at the approaching soldiers, his face carved with the lines of fury and scorn.

"What is it?" Amanda asked.

I had been as baffled as the rest. Then a faint sound came to my ear. The regiments were at last close enough to be heard; and what we were hearing were their regimental bands—except Michael's band, of course—as a faint snatch of melody on the breeze. It was barely hearable, but I recognized it, as El Conde obviously already had.

"They're playing the *te guelo*," I said. "Announcing '*no quarter.*' "

The *te guelo* is a promise to cut the throat of anyone opposing. Amanda's eyebrows rose.

"For us?" she said. "What good do they think that's going to do?"

"They may think Michael's bandsmen are still with us, and perhaps they're hoping to scare them out," I said. "But probably they're doing it just because it's always done when they attack."

The others listened for a second. The *te guelo* is an effectively chilling piece of music; but, as Amanda had implied, it was a little beside the point to play it to Dorsai who had already made their decision to fight.

"Where's Michael?" she asked now.

I looked around. It was a good question. If he had indeed gone for weapons, he should have been back out on the terrace by this time. But there was no sign of him.

"I don't know," I said.

"They've stopped their portable weapons," Kensie said, "and they're setting them up to fire. Still out of effective range, against walls like this."

"We'd probably be better down behind the armor of our own embayments and ready to fire back when they get a little closer," said Ian. "They can't hurt the walls from where they are. They might get lucky and hurt some of us."

He turned to El Conde.

"If you'd care to step down into one of the weapon embayments, sir—" he said.

El Conde shook his head.

"I shall watch from here," he announced.

Ian nodded. He looked at Padma.

"Of course," said Padma. "I'll come in with one of you—unless I can be useful in some other way?"

"No," said Ian. A shouting from the approaching soldiers that drowned out the band music turned him and the rest of us once more toward the plain.

The front line of the attackers had broken into a run toward us. They were only a hundred meters or so now from the foot of the slope leading to the walls of Gebel Nahar. Whether it had been decided that they should attack from that distance, or—more likely—someone had been carried away and started forward early, did not matter. The attack had begun.

For a moment, all of us who knew combat recognized immediately, this development had given us a temporary respite from the portable weapons. With their own soldiers flooding out ahead, it would be difficult for the gunners to fire at Gebel Nahar without killing their own men. It was the sort of small happenstance that can sometimes be turned to an advantage—but, as I stared out at the plain, I had no idea of what we might do that in that moment that would make any real difference to the battle's outcome.

"Look!"

It was Amanda calling. The shouting of the attacking soldiers had stopped, suddenly. She was standing right at the parapet, pointing out and down. I took one step forward, so that I could see the slope below close by the foot of the first wall, and saw what she had seen.

The front line of the attackers was full of men trying to slow down against the continued pressure of those behind who had not yet seen what those in front had. The result was effectively a halting of the attack as more and more of them stared at what was happening on the slope.

What was happening there was that the lid of El Conde's private exit from Gebel Nahar was rising. To the Naharese military it must have looked as if some secret weapon was about to unveil itself on the slope—and it would have been this that had caused them to have sudden doubts and their front line of men to dig in their heels. They were still a good two or three hundred meters from the tunnel entrance, and the first line of attackers, trapped where they were by those behind them, must have suddenly conceived of themselves as sitting ducks for whatever field-class weapon would elevate itself through this unexpected opening and zero in on them.

But of course no such weapon came out. Instead, what emerged was what looked like a head wearing a regimental cap, with a stick tilted back by its right ear . . . and slowly, up on to the level of the ground, and out to face them all came Michael.

He was still without weapons. But he was now dressed in his full parade regimentals as band officer; and the *gaita gallega* was resting in his arms and on his shoulder, the mouthpiece between his lips, the long drone over his shoulder. He stepped out on to the slope of the hill and began to march down it, toward the Naharese.

The silence was deadly; and into that silence, striking up, came the sound of the *gaita gallega* as he started to play it. Clear and strong it came to us on the wall; and clearly it reached as well to the now-silent and motionless ranks of the Naharese. He was playing *Su Madre*.

He went forward at a march step, shoulders level; the instrument held securely in his arms; and his playing went before him, throwing its challenge directly into their faces. A single figure marching against six thousand.

From where I stood, I had a slight angle on him; and with the help of the magnification of the screen on the watch camera next to me, I could get just a glimpse of his face from the side and behind him. He looked peaceful and intent. The exhausted leanness and tension I had seen in him earlier seemed to have gone out of him. He marched as if on parade, with the intentness of a good musician in performance, and all the time *Su Madre* was hooting and mocking at the armed regiments before him.

I touched the controls of the camera to make it give me a closeup look at the men in the front of the Naharese force. They stood as if paralyzed, as I panned along their line. They were saying nothing, doing nothing, only watching Michael come toward them as if he meant to march right through them. All along their front, they were stopped and watching.

But their inaction was something that could not last—a moment of shock that had to wear off. Even as I watched, they began to stir and speak. Michael was between us and them, and with the incredible voice of the bagpipe his notes came almost loudly to our ears. But rising behind them, we now began to hear a low-pitched swell of sound like the growl of some enormous beast.

I looked in the screen. The regiments were still not advancing, but none of the figures I now saw as I panned down the front were standing frozen with shock. In the middle of the crescent formation, the soldiers of the Guard Regiment who held a feud with

Michael's own Third Regiment, were shaking weapons and fists at him and shouting. I had no way of knowing what they were saying, at this distance, and the camera could not help me with that, but I had no doubt that they were answering challenge with challenge, insult with insult.

All along the line, the front boiled, becoming more active every minute. They had all seen that Michael was unarmed; and for a few moments this held them in check. They threatened, but did not offer to, fire on him. But even at this distance I could feel the fury building up in them. It was only a matter of time, I thought, until one of them lost his self-control and used the weapon he carried.

I wanted to shout at Michael to turn around and come back to the tunnel. He had broken the momentum of their attack and thrown them into confusion. With troops like this they would certainly not take up their advance where they had halted it. It was almost a certainty that after this challenge, this emotional shock, that their senior officers would pull them back and reform them before coming on again. A valuable breathing space had been gained. It could be some hours, it could be not until tomorrow they would be able to mount a second attack; and in that time internal tensions or any number of developments might work to help us further. Michael still had them between his thumb and forefinger. If he turned his back on them now, their inaction might well hold until he was back in safety.

But there was no way I could reach him with that message. And he showed no intention of turning back on his own. Instead he went steadily forward, scorning them with his music, taunting them for attacking in their numbers an opponent so much less than themselves.

Still the Naharese soldiery only shook their weapons and shouted insults at him; but now in the screen I began to see a difference. On the wing occupied by the Third Regiment there were uniformed figures beginning to wave Michael back. I moved the view of the screen further out along that wing and saw individuals in civilian clothes, some of those from the following swarm of volunteers and revolutionaries, who were pushing their way to the front, kneeling down and putting weapons to their shoulders.

The Third Regiment soldiers were pushing these others back and jerking their weapons away from them. Fights were beginning to break out; but on that wing, those who wished to fire on Michael were being held back. It was plain that the Third Regiment was torn now between its commitment to join in the attack on Gebel Nahar and its impulse to protect their former bandmaster in his act of outrageous bravery. Still, I saw one civilian with the starved face of a fanatic who had literally to be tackled and held on the ground by three of the Third Regiment before he could be stopped from firing on Michael.

A sudden cold suspicion passed through me. I swung the view of the screen to the opposite wing; and there I saw the same situation. From behind the uniformed soldiers there, volunteers and civilian revolutionaries were trying to stop Michael with their weapons. Some undoubtedly were from the neighboring principalities where a worship of drama and acts of flamboyant courage was not part of the culture, as it was here. On this wing, also, the soldiers were trying to stop those individuals who attempted to shoot Michael. But here, the effort to prevent that firing was scattered and ineffective.

I saw a number of weapons of all types leveled at Michael. No sound could reach me, and only the sport guns and ancient explosive weapons showed any visible sign that they were being fired; but it was clear that death was finally in the air around Michael.

I switched the view hastily back to him. For a moment he continued to march forward in the screen as if some invisible armor was protecting him. Then he stumbled slightly, caught himself, went forward, and fell.

For a second time—for a moment only—the voice of the attackers stopped, cut off as if a multitude of invisible hands had been clapped over the mouths of those there. I lifted the view on the screen from the fallen shape of Michael and saw soldiers and civilians alike standing motionless, staring at him, as if they could not believe that he had at last been brought down.

Then, on the wing opposite to that held by the Third Regiment, the civilians that had been firing began to dance and wave their weapons in the air—and suddenly the whole formation seemed to collapse inward, the two wings melting back into the main body as the soldiers of the Third Regiment charged across the front to get at the rejoicing civilians, and the Guard Regiment swirled out to oppose them. The fighting spread as individual attacked individual. In a moment they were all embroiled. A wild mob without direction or purpose of any kind, except to kill whoever was closest, took the place of the military formation that had existed only five minutes before.

As the fighting became general, the tight mass of bodies spread out like butter rapidly melting down from a solid to a liquid; and the struggle spread out over a larger and larger area, until at last it covered even the place where Michael had fallen. Amanda turned away from the parapet and I caught her as she staggered. I held her upright and she leaned heavily against me.

"I have to lie down, I guess," she murmured.

I led her towards the door and the bed that was waiting for her back in the medical section. Ian, Kensie and Padma turned and followed, leaving only El Conde, leaning on his silver-headed stick and staring out at what was taking place on the plain, his face lighted with the fierce satisfaction of a hawk perched above the body of its kill.

It was twilight before all the fighting had ceased; and, with the dark, there began to be heard the small sounds of the annunciator chimes at the main gate. One by one Michael's bandsmen began to slip back to us in Gebel Nahar. With their return, Ian, Kensie and I were able to stop taking turns at standing watch, as we had up until then. But it was not until after midnight that we felt it was safe to leave long enough to go out and recover Michael's body.

Amanda insisted on going with us. There was no reason to argue against her coming with us and a good deal of reason in favor of it. She was responding very well to the drainage unit and a further eight hours of sleep had rebuilt her strength to a remarkable degree. Also, she was the one who suggested we take Michael's body back to the Dorsai for burial.

The cost of travel between the worlds was such that few individuals could afford it; and few Dorsai who died in the course of their duties off-planet had their bodies returned for interment in native soil. But we had adequate space to carry Michael's body with us in the courier vessel; and it was Amanda's point that Michael had solved the problem by his action— something for which the Dorsai world in general owed him a debt. Both Padma and El Conde had agreed, after what had happened today, that the Naharese would not be brought back to the idea of revolution again for some time. William's machinations had fallen through. Ian and Kensie could now either make it their choice to stay and execute their contract, or legitimately withdraw from it for the reason that they had been faced with situations beyond their control.

In the end, all of us except Padma went out to look for Michael's body, leaving the returned bandsmen to stand duty. It was full night by the time we emerged once more on to the plain through the secret exit.

"El Conde will have to have another of these made for him," commented Kensie, as we came out under the star-brilliant sky. "This passage is more a national monument than a secret, now."

The night was one very much like the one before, when Kensie and I had made our sweep in search of observers from the other side. But this time we were looking only for the dead; and that was all we found.

During the afternoon all the merely wounded had been taken away by their friends; but there were bodies to be seen as we moved out to the spot where we had seen Michael go down, but not many of them. It had been possible to mark the location exactly using the surveying equipment built into the watch cameras. But the bodies were not many. The fighting had been more a weaponed brawl than a battle. Which did not alter the fact that those who had died were dead. They would not come to life again, any more than Michael would. A small night breeze touched our faces from time to time as we walked. It was too soon after the fighting for the odors of death to have taken possession of the battlefield. For the present moment under the stars the scene we saw, including the dead bodies, had all the neatness and antiseptic quality of a stage setting.

We came to the place where Michael's body should have been, but it was gone. Ian switched on a pocket lamp; and he, with Kensie, squatted to examine the ground. I waited with Amanda. Ian and Kensie were the experienced field officers, with Hunter Team practise. I could spend several hours looking, to see what they would take in at a glance.

After a few minutes they stood up again and Ian switched off the lamp. There were a few seconds while our eyes readjusted, and then the plain became real around us once more, replacing the black wall of darkness that the lamplight had instantly created.

"He was here, all right," Kensie said. "Evidently

quite a crowd came to carry his body off someplace else. It'll be easy enough to follow the way they went."

We followed the trail of scuffed earth and broken vegetation left by the footwear of those who had carried away Michael's body. The track they had left was plain enough so that I myself had no trouble picking it out, even by starlight, as we went along at a walk. It led further away from Gebel Nahar, toward where the center of the Naharese formation had been when the general fighting broke out; and as we went, bodies became more numerous. Eventually, at a spot which must have been close to where the Guard Regiment had stood, we found Michael.

The mound on which his body lay was visible as a dark mass in the starlight, well before we reached it. But it was only when Ian switched on his pocket lamp again that we saw its true identity and purpose. It was a pile nearly a meter in height and a good two meters long and broad. Most of what made it up was clothes; but there were many other things mixed in with the cloth items—belts and ornamental chains, ancient weapons, so old that they must have been heirlooms, bits of personal jewelry, even shoes and boots.

But, as I say, the greater part of what made it up was clothing—in particular uniform jackets or shirts, although a fair number of detached sleeves or collars bearing insignia of rank had evidently been deliberately torn off by their owners and added as separate items.

On top of all this, lying on his back with his dead

face turned toward the stars, was Michael. I did not need an interpretation of what I was seeing here, after my earlier look at the painting in the Nahar City Spaceport Terminal. Michael lay not with a sword, but with the *gaita gallega* held to his chest; and beneath him was the *leto de muerte*—the real *leto de muerte*, made up of everything that those who had seen him there that day, and who had fought for and against him after it was too late, considered the most valuable thing they could give from what was in their possession at the time.

Each had given the best he could, to build up a bed of state for the dead hero—a bed of triumph, actually, for in winning here Michael had won everything, according to their rules and their ways. After the supreme victory of his courage, as they saw it, there was nothing left for them but the offering of tribute; their possessions or their lives.

We stood, we four, looking at it all in silence. Finally, Kensie spoke.

"Do you still want to take him home?"

"No," said Amanda. The word was almost as a sigh from her, as she stood looking at the dead Michael. "No. This is his home, now."

We went back to Gebel Nahar, leaving the corpse of Michael with its honor guard of the other dead around him.

The next day Amanda and I left Gebel Nahar to return to the Dorsai. Kensie and Ian had decided to complete their contract; and it looked as if they should be able to do so without difficulty. With dawn, individual soldiers of the regiments had begun pouring back into Gebel Nahar, asking to be accepted once more into their duties. They were eager to please, and for Naharese, remarkably subdued.

Padma was also leaving. He rode into the spaceport with us, as did Kensie and Ian, who had come along to see us off. In the terminal, we stopped to look once more at the *leto de muerte* painting.

"Now I understand," said Amanda, after a moment. She turned from the painting and lightly touched both Ian and Kensie who were standing on either side of her.

"We'll be back," she said, and led the two of them off.

I was left with Padma.

"Understand?" I said to him. "The *leto de muerte* concept?"

"No," said Padma, softly. "I think she meant that now she understands what Michael came to understand, and how it applies to her. How it applies to everyone, including me and you."

I felt coldness on the back of my neck.

"To me?" I said.

"You have lost part of your protection, the armor of your sorrow and loss," he answered. "To a certain extent, when you let yourself become concerned with Michael's problem, you let someone else in to touch you again."

I looked at him, a little grimly.

"You think so?" I put the matter aside. "I've got to get out and start the checkover on the ship. Why don't you come along? When Amanda and the others come back and don't find us here, they'll know where to look."

Padma shook his head.

"I'm afraid I'd better say goodby now," he replied. "There are other urgencies that have been demanding my attention for some time and I've put them aside for this. Now, it's time to pay them some attention. So I'll say goodby now; and you can give my farewells to the others."

"Goodby, then," I said.

As when we had met, he did not offer me his hand; but the warmth of him struck through to me; and for the first time I faced the possibility that perhaps he was right. That Michael, or he, or Amanda—or perhaps the whole affair—had either worn thin a spot, or chipped off a piece, of that shell that had closed around me when I watched them kill Else.

"Perhaps we'll run into each other again," I said.

"With people like ourselves," he said, "it's very likely."

He smiled once more, turned and went.

I crossed the terminal to the Security Section, identified myself and went out to the courier ship. It was no more than half an hour's work to run the checkover—these special vessels are practically self-monitoring. When I finished the others had still not yet appeared. I was about to go in search of them when Amanda pulled herself through the open entrance port and closed it behind her.

"Where's Kensie and Ian?" I asked.

"They were paged. The Board of Governors

showed up at Gebel Nahar, without warning. They both had to hurry back for a full-dress confrontation. I told them I'd say goodby to you for them."

"All right. Padma sends his farewells by me to the rest of you."

She laughed and sat down in the copilot's seat beside me.

"I'll have to write Ian and Kensie to pass Padma's on," she said. "Are we ready to lift?"

"As soon as we're cleared for it. That port sealed?"

She nodded. I reached out to the instrument bank before me, keyed Traffic Control and asked to be put in sequence for liftoff. Then I gave my attention to the matter of warming the bird to life.

Thirty-five minutes later we lifted, and another ten minutes after that saw us safely clear of the atmosphere. I headed out for the legally requisite number of planetary diameters before making the first phase shift. Then, finally, with mind and hands free, I was able to turn my attention again to Amanda.

She was lost in thought, gazing deep into the pinpoint fires of the visible stars in the navigation screen above the instrument bank. I watched her without speaking for a moment, thinking again that Padma had possibly been right. Earlier, even when she had spoken to me in the dark of my room of how she felt about Ian, I had touched nothing of her. But now, I could feel the life in her as she sat beside me.

She must have sensed my eyes on her, because she roused from her private consultation with the stars and looked over.

"Something on your mind?" she asked.

"No," I said. "Or rather, yes. I didn't really follow your thinking, back in the terminal when we were looking at the painting and you said that now you understood."

"You didn't?" She watched me for a fraction of a second. "I meant that now I understood what Michael had."

"Padma said he thought you'd meant you understood how it applied to you—and to everyone."

She did not answer for a second.

"You're wondering about me—and Ian and Kensie," she said.

"It's not important what I wonder," I said.

"Yes, it is. After all, I dumped the whole matter in your lap in the first place, without warning. It's going to be all right. They'll finish up their contract here and then Ian will go to Earth for Leah. They'll be married and she'll settle in Foralie."

"And Kensie?"

"Kensie." She smiled sadly. "Kensie'll go on . . . his own way."

"And you?"

"I'll go mine." She looked at me very much as Padma had looked at me, as we stood below the painting. "That's what I meant when I said I'd understood. In the end the only way is to be what you are and do what you must. If you do that, everything works. Michael found that out."

"And threw his life away putting it into practice."

"No," she said swiftly. "He threw nothing away. There were only two things he wanted. One was to be the Dorsai he was born to be and the other was never to use a weapon; and it seemed he could have either one but not the other. Only, he was true to both and it worked. In the end, he was Dorsai and unarmed—and by being both he stopped an army."

Her eyes held me so powerfully that I could not look away.

"He went his way and found his life," she said, "and my answer is to go mine. Ian, his. And Kensie, his—"

She broke off so abruptly I knew what she had been about to say.

"Give me time," I said; and the words came a little more thickly than I had expected. "It's too soon yet. Still too soon since she died. But give me time, and maybe . . . maybe, even me."

●

WARRIOR

The spaceliner coming in from New Earth and Freiland, worlds under the Sirian sun, was delayed in its landing by traffic at the spaceport in Long Island Sound. The two police lieutenants, waiting on the bare concrete beyond the shelter of the Terminal buildings, turned up the collars of their cloaks against the hissing sleet, in this unweatherproofed area. The sleet was turning into tiny hailstones that bit and stung all exposed areas of skin. The gray November sky poured them down without pause or mercy; the vast, reaching surface of concrete seemed to dance with their white multitudes.

"Here it comes now," said Tyburn, the Manhattan Complex police lieutenant, risking a glance up into the hailstorm. "Let me do the talking when we take him in."

"Fine by me," answered Breagan, the spaceport officer, "I'm only here to introduce you—and because it's my bailiwick. You can have Kenebuck, with his hood connections, and his millions. If it were up to me, I'd let the soldier get him."

"It's him," said Tyburn, "who's likely to get the soldier—and that's why I'm here. You ought to know that."

The great mass of the interstellar ship settled like a cautious mountain to the concrete two hundred yards off. It protruded a landing stair near its base like a metal leg, and the passengers began to disembark. The two policemen spotted their man immediately in the crowd.

"He's big," said Breagan, with the judicious ap-

praisal of someone safely on the sidelines, as the two
of them moved forward.

"They're all big, these professional military men
off the Dorsai world," answered Tyburn, a little irri-
tably, shrugging his shoulders against the cold, under
his cloak. "They breed themselves that way."

"I know they're big," said Breagan. "This one's
bigger."

The first wave of passengers was rolling toward
them now, their quarry among the mass. Tyburn and
Breagan moved forward to meet him. When they got
close they could see, even through the hissing sleet,
every line of his dark, unchanging face looming
above the lesser heights of the people around him,
his military erectness molding the civilian clothes he
wore until they might as well have been a uniform.
Tyburn found himself staring fixedly at the tall figure
as it came toward him. He had met such professional
soldiers from the Dorsai before, and the stamp of
their breeding had always been plain on them. But
this man was somehow more so, even than the others
Tyburn had seen. In some way he seemed to be the
spirit of the Dorsai, incarnate.

He was one of twin brothers, Tyburn remembered
now from the dossier back at his office. Ian and
Kensie were their names, of the Graeme family at
Foralie, on the Dorsai. And the report was that
Kensie had two men's likability, while his brother
Ian, now approaching Tyburn, had a double portion
of grim shadow and solitary darkness.

Staring at the man coming toward him, Tyburn
could believe the dossier now. For a moment, even,

with the sleet and the cold taking possession of him, he found himself believing in the old saying that, if the born soldiers of the Dorsai ever cared to pull back to their own small, rocky world, and challenge the rest of humanity, not all the thirteen other inhabited planets could stand against them. Once, Tyburn had laughed at that idea. Now, watching Ian approach, he could not laugh. A man like this would live for different reasons from those of ordinary men—and die for different reasons.

Tyburn shook off the wild notion. The figure coming toward him, he reminded himself sharply, was a professional military man—nothing more.

Ian was almost to them now. The two policemen moved in through the crowd and intercepted him.

"Commandant Ian Graeme?" said Breagan. "I'm Kaj Breagan of the spaceport police. This is Lieutenant Walter Tyburn of the Manhattan Complex Force. I wonder if you could give us a few minutes of your time?"

Ian Graeme nodded, almost indifferently. He turned and paced along with them, his longer stride making more leisurely work of their brisk walking, as they led him away from the route of the disembarking passengers and in through a blank metal door at one end of the Terminal, marked *Unauthorized Entry Prohibited*. Inside, they took an elevator tube up to the offices on the Terminal's top floor, and ended up in chairs around a desk in one of the offices.

All the way in, Ian had said nothing. He sat in his chair now with the same indifferent patience, gazing at Tyburn, behind the desk, and at Breagan, seated back against the wall at the desk's right side. Tyburn found himself staring back in fascination. Not at the granite face, but at the massive, powerful hands of the man, hanging idly between the chair-arms that supported his forearms. Tyburn, with an effort, wrenched his gaze from those hands.

"Well, Commandant," he said, forcing himself at last to look up into the dark, unchanging features, "you're here on Earth for a visit, we understand."

"To see the next-of-kin of an officer of mine." Ian's voice, when he spoke at last, was almost mild compared to the rest of his appearance. It was a deep, calm voice, but lightless—like a voice that had long forgotten the need to be angry or threatening. Only ... there was something sad about it, Tyburn thought.

"A James Kenebuck?" said Tyburn.

"That's right," answered the deep voice of Ian. "His younger brother, Brian Kenebuck, was on my staff in the recent campaign on Freiland. He died three months back."

"Do you," said Tyburn, "always visit your deceased officers' next of kin?"

"When possible. Usually, of course, they die in the line of duty."

"I see," said Tyburn. The office chair in which he sat seemed hard and uncomfortable underneath him. He shifted slightly. "You don't happen to be armed, do you, Commandant?"

Ian did not even smile.

"No," he said.

"Of course, of course," said Tyburn, uncomfortable. "Not that it makes any difference." He was looking again, in spite of himself, at the two massive, relaxed hands opposite him. "Your . . . extremities by themselves are lethal weapons. We register professional karate and boxing experts here, you know—or did you know?"

Ian nodded.

"Yes," said Tyburn. He wet his lips, and then was furious with himself for doing so. Damn my orders, he thought suddenly and whitely, I don't have to sit here making a fool of myself in front of this man, no matter how many connections and millions Kenebuck owns.

"All right, look here, Commandant," he said, harshly, leaning forward. "We've had a communication from the Freiland-North Police about you. They suggest that you hold Kenebuck—James Kenebuck—responsible for his brother Brian's death."

Ian sat looking back at him without answering.

"Well," demanded Tyburn, raggedly after a long moment, "do you?"

"Force-leader Brian Kenebuck," said Ian calmly, "led his Force, consisting of thirty-six men at the time, against orders, farther than was wise into enemy perimeter. His Force was surrounded and badly shot up. Only he and four men returned to the lines. He was brought to trial in the field under the Mercenaries Code for deliberate mishandling of his troops under combat conditions. The four men who had returned with him testified against him. He was found guilty and I ordered him shot."

Ian stopped speaking. His voice had been perfectly even, but there was so much finality about the way he spoke that after he finished there was a pause in the room while Tyburn and Breagan stared at him as if they had both been tranced. Then the silence, echoing in Tyburn's ears, jolted him back to life.

"I don't see what all this has to do with James Kenebuck, then," said Tyburn. "Brian committed some ... military crime, and was executed for it. You say you gave the order. If anyone's responsible for Brian Kenebuck's death then, it seems to me it'd be you. Why connect it with someone who wasn't even there at the time, someone who was here on Earth all the while, James Kenebuck?"

"Brian," said Ian, "was his brother."

The emotionless statement was calm and coldly reasonable in the silent, brightly-lit office. Tyburn found his open hands had shrunk themselves into fists on the desk top. He took a deep breath and began to speak in a flat, official tone.

"Commandant," he said, "I don't pretend to understand you. You're a man of the Dorsai, a product of one of the splinter cultures out among the stars. I'm just an old-fashioned Earthborn—but I'm a policeman in the Manhattan Complex and James Kenebuck is ... well, he's a taxpayer in the Manhattan Complex."

He found he was talking without meeting Ian's eyes. He forced himself to look at them—they were dark unmoving eyes.

"It's my duty to inform you," Tyburn went on, "that we've had intimations to the effect that you're to

bring some retribution to James Kenebuck, because
of Brian Kenebuck's death. These are only intimations, and as long as you don't break any laws here
on Earth, you're free to go where you want and see
whom you like. But this *is Earth, Commandant*."

He paused, hoping that Ian would make some sound,
some movement. But Ian only sat there, waiting.

"We don't have any Mercenaries Code here, Commandant," Tyburn went on harshly. "We haven't any
feud-right, no *droit-de-main*. But we do have laws.
Those laws say that, though a man may be the worst
murderer alive, until he's brought to book in our
courts, under our process of laws, no one is allowed
to harm a hair of his head. Now, I'm not here to argue whether this is the best way or not; just to tell
you that that's the way things are." Tyburn stared fixedly into the dark eyes. "Now," he said, bluntly, "I
know that if you're determined to try to kill Kenebuck without counting the cost, I can't prevent it."

He paused and waited again. But Ian still said
nothing.

"I know," said Tyburn, "that you can walk up to
him like any other citizen, and once you're within
reach you can try to kill him with your bare hands
before anyone can stop you. *I* can't stop you in that
case. But what I can do is catch you afterwards, if
you succeed, and see you convicted and executed for
murder. And you *will* be caught and convicted,
there's no doubt about it. You can't kill James
Kenebuck the way someone like you would kill a
man, and get away with it here on Earth—do you understand that, Commandant?"

"Yes," said Ian.

"All right," said Tyburn, letting out a deep breath. "Then you understand. You're a sane man and a Dorsai professional. From what I've been able to learn about the Dorsai, it's one of your military tenets that part of a man's duty to himself is not to throw his life away in a hopeless cause. And this cause of your to bring Kenebuck to justice for his brother's death, is hopeless."

He stopped. Ian straightened in a movement preliminary to getting up.

"Wait a second," said Tyburn.

He had come to the hard part of the interview. He had prepared his speech for this moment and rehearsed it over and over again—but now he found himself without faith that it would convince Ian.

"One more word," said Tyburn. "You're a man of camps and battlefields, a man of the military; and you must be used to thinking of yourself as a pretty effective individual. But here, on Earth, those special skills of yours are mostly illegal. And without them you're ineffective and helpless. Kenebuck, on the other hand, is just the opposite. He's got money—millions. And he's got connections, some of them nasty. And he was born and raised here in Manhattan Complex." Tyburn stared emphatically at the tall, dark man, willing him to understand. "Do you follow me? If you, for example, should suddenly turn up dead here, we just might not be able to bring Kenebuck to book for it. Where we absolutely could, and would, bring you to book if the situation were reversed. Think about it."

He sat, still staring at Ian. But Ian's face showed no change, or sign that the message had gotten through to him.

"Thank you," Ian said. "If there's nothing more, I'll be going."

"There's nothing more," said Tyburn, defeated. He watched Ian leave. It was only when Ian was gone, and he turned back to Breagan that he recovered a little of his self-respect. For Breagan's face had paled.

Ian went down through the Terminal and took a cab into Manhattan Complex, to the John Adams Hotel. He registered for a room on the fourteenth floor of the transient section of that hotel and inquired about the location of James Kenebuck's suite in the resident section; then sent his card up to Kenebuck with a request to come by to see the millionaire. After that, he went on up to his own room, unpacked his luggage, which had already been delivered from the spaceport, and took out a small, sealed package. Just at that moment there was a soft chiming sound and his card was returned to him from a delivery slot in the room wall. It fell into the salver below the slot and he picked it up, to read what was written on the face of it. The penciled note read:

Come on up—
        K.

He tucked the card and the package into a pocket and left his transient room. And Tyburn, who had followed him to the hotel, and who had been observing all of Ian's actions from the second of his arrival, through sensors placed in the walls and ceilings, half rose from his chair in the room of the empty suite directly above Kenebuck's which had been quietly taken over as a police observation post. Then, helplessly, Tyburn swore and sat down again, to follow Ian's movements in the screen fed by the sensors. So far there was nothing the policeman could do legally—nothing but watch.

So he watched as Ian strode down the softly carpeted hallway to the elevator tube, rose in it to the eightieth floor and stepped out to face the heavy, transparent door sealing off the resident section of the hotel. He held up the card with Kenebuck's message to a concierge screen beside the door, and with a soft sigh of air the door slid back to let him through. He passed on in, found a second elevator tube, and took it up thirteen more stories. Black doors opened before him—and he stepped one step forward into a small foyer to find himself surrounded by three men.

They were big men—one, a lantern-jawed giant, was even bigger than Ian—and they were vicious. Tyburn, watching through the sensor in the foyer ceiling that had been secretly placed there by the police the day before, recognized all of them from his files. They were underworld muscle hired by Kenebuck at word of Ian's coming; all armed, and brutal and hairtrigger—mad dogs of the lower city. After that first step into their midst, Ian stood still. And there followed a strange, unnatural cessation of movement in the room.

The three stood checked. They had been about to put their hands on Ian to search him for something, Tyburn saw, and probably to rough him up in the process. But something had stopped them, some abrupt change in the air around them. Tyburn, watching, felt the change as they did; but for a moment he felt it without understanding. Then understanding came to him.

The difference was in Ian, in the way he stood there. He was, saw Tyburn, simply . . . waiting. That same patient indifference Tyburn had seen upon him in the Terminal office was there again. In the split second of his single step into the room he had discovered the men, had measured them, and stopped. Now, he waited, in his turn, for one of them to make a move.

A sort of black lightning had entered the small foyer. It was abruptly obvious to the watching Tyburn, as to the three below, that the first of them to lay hands on Ian would be the first to find the hands of the Dorsai soldier upon him—and those hands were death.

For the first time in his life, Tyburn saw the personal power of the Dorsai fighting man, made plain without words. Ian needed no badge upon him, standing as he stood now, to warn that he was dangerous. The men about him were mad dogs; but, patently, Ian was a wolf. There was a difference with the three, which Tyburn now recognized for the first time. Dogs—even mad dogs—fight, and the losing dog, if he can, runs away. But no wolf runs. For a wolf wins every fight but one, and in that one he dies.

After a moment, when it was clear that none of the three would move, Ian stepped forward. He passed through them without even brushing against one of them, to the inner door opposite, and opened it and went on through.

He stepped into a three-level living room stretching to a large, wide window, its glass rolled up, and black with the sleet-filled night. The living room was as large as a small suite in itself, and filled with people, men and women, richly dressed. They held cocktail glasses in their hands as they stood or sat, and talked. The atmosphere was heavy with the scents of alcohol, and women's perfumes and cigarette smoke. It seemed that they paid no attention to his entrance, but their eyes followed him covertly once he had passed.

He walked forward through the crowd, picking his way to a figure before the dark window, the figure of a man almost as tall as himself, erect, athletic-looking with a handsome, sharp-cut face under whitish-blond hair that stared at Ian with a sort of incredulity as Ian approached.

"Graeme . . . ?" said this man, as Ian stopped before him. His voice in this moment of off-guardedness betrayed its two levels, the semi-hoodlum whine and harshness underneath, the polite accents above. "My boys . . . you didn't—" he stumbled, "leave anything with them when you were coming in?"

"No," said Ian. "You're James Kenebuck, of

course. You look like your brother." Kenebuck stared at him.

"Just a minute," he said. He set down his glass, turned and went quickly through the crowd and into the foyer, shutting the door behind him. In the hush of the room, those there heard, first silence than a short, unintelligible burst of sharp voices, then silence again. Kenebuck came back into the room, two spots of angry color high on his cheekbones. He came back to face Ian.

"Yes," he said, halting before Ian. "They were supposed to . . . tell me when you came in." He fell silent, evidently waiting for Ian to speak, but Ian merely stood, examining him, until the spots of color on Kenebuck's cheekbones flared again.

"Well?" he said, abruptly. "Well? You came here to see me about Brian, didn't you? What about Brian?" He added, before Ian could answer, in a tone suddenly brutal: "I know he was shot, so you don't have to break that news to me. I suppose you want to tell me he showed all sorts of noble guts—refused a blindfold and that sort of—"

"No," said Ian. "He didn't die nobly."

Kenebuck's tall, muscled body jerked a little at the words, almost as if the bullets of an invisible firing squad had poured into it.

"Well . . . that's fine!" he laughed angrily. "You come light-years to see me and then you tell me that! I thought you liked him—liked Brian."

"Liked him? No," Ian shook his head. Kenebuck stiffened, his face for a moment caught in a gape of bewilderment. "As a matter of fact," went on Ian, "he was a glory-hunter. That made him a poor soldier and a worse officer. I'd have transferred him out of my command if I'd had time before the campaign on Freiland started. Because of him, we lost the lives of thirty-two men in his Force, that night."

"Oh," Kenebuck pulled himself together, and looked sourly at Ian. "Those thirty-two men. You've got them on your conscience—is that it?"

"No," said Ian. There was no emphasis on the word as he said it, but somehow to Tyburn's ears above, the brief short negative dismissed Kenebuck's question with an abruptness like contempt. The spots of color on Kenebuck's cheeks flamed.

"You didn't like Brian and your conscience doesn't bother you—what're you here for, then?" he snapped.

"My duty brings me," said Ian.

"Duty?" Kenebuck's face stilled, and went rigid.

Ian reached slowly into his pocket as if he were surrendering a weapon under the guns of an enemy and did not want his move misinterpreted. He brought out the package from his pocket.

"I brought you Brian's personal effects," he said. He turned and laid the package on a table beside Kenebuck. Kenebuck stared down at the package and the color over his cheekbones faded until his face was nearly as pale as his hair. Then slowly, hesitantly, as if he were approaching a booby-trap, he reached out and gingerly picked it up. He held it and turned to Ian, staring into Ian's eyes, almost demandingly.

"It's in here?" said Kenebuck, in a voice barely above a whisper, and with a strange emphasis.

"Brian's effects," said Ian, watching him.

"Yes . . . sure. All right," said Kenebuck. He was plainly trying to pull himself together, but his voice was still almost whispering. "I guess . . . that settles it."

"That settles it," said Ian. Their eyes held together. "Good-by," said Ian. He turned and walked back through the silent crowd and out of the living room. The three muscle-men were no longer in the foyer. He took the elevator tube down and returned to his own hotel room.

Tyburn, who with a key to the service elevators, had not had to change tubes on the way down as Ian had, was waiting for him when Ian entered. Ian did not seem surprised to see Tyburn there, and only glanced casually at the policeman as he crossed to a decanter of Dorsai whisky that had since been delivered up to the room.

"That's that, then!" burst out Tyburn, in relief. "You got in to see him and he ended up letting you out. You can pack up and go, now. It's over."

"No," said Ian. "Nothing's over yet." He poured a few inches of the pungent, dark whisky into a glass, and moved the decanter over another glass. "Drink?"

"I'm on duty," said Tyburn, sharply.

"There'll be a little wait," said Ian, calmly. He poured some whisky into the other glass, took up both glasses, and stepped across the room to hand one to Tyburn. Tyburn found himself holding it. Ian had stepped on to stand before the wall-high window. Outside, night had fallen; but—faintly seen in the light from the city levels below—the sleet here above the weather shield still beat like small, dark ghosts against the transparency.

"Hang it, man, what more do you want?" burst out Tyburn. "Can't you see it's you I'm trying to protect—as well as Kenebuck? I don't want *anyone* killed! If you stay around here now, you're asking for it. I keep telling you, here in Manhattan Complex you're the helpless one, not Kenebuck. Do you think he hasn't made plans to take care of you?"

"Not until he's sure," said Ian, turning from the ghost-sleet, beating like lost souls against the window-glass, trying to get in.

"Sure about what? Look, Commandant," said Tyburn, trying to speak calmly, "half an hour after we heard from the Freiland-North Police about you, Kenebuck called my office to ask for police protection." He broke off, angrily. "Don't look at me like that! How do I know how he found out you were coming? I tell you he's rich, and he's got connections! But the point is, the police protection he's got is just a screen—an excuse—for whatever he's got planned for you on his own. You saw those hoods in the foyer!"

"Yes," said Ian, unemotionally.

"Well, think about it!" Tyburn glared at him. "Look, I don't hold any brief for James Kenebuck! All right—let me tell you about him! We knew he'd been trying to get rid of his brother since Brian was ten—but blast it, Commandant, Brian was no angel, either—"

"I know," said Ian, seating himself in a chair opposite Tyburn.

"All right, you know! I'll tell you anyway!" said Tyburn. "Their grandfather was a local kingpin—he was in every racket on the eastern seaboard. He was one of the mob, with millions he didn't dare count because of where they'd come from. In their father's time, those millions started to be fed into legitimate businesses. The third generation, James and Brian, didn't inherit anything that wasn't legitimate. Hell, we couldn't even make a jaywalking ticket stick against one of them, if we'd ever wanted to. James was twenty and Brian ten when their father died, and when he died the last bit of tattle-tale gray went out of the family linen. But they kept their hoodlum connections, Commandant!"

Ian sat, glass in hand, watching Tyburn almost curiously.

"Don't you get it?" snapped Tyburn. "I tell you that, on paper, in law, Kenebuck's twenty-four carat gilt-edge. But his family was hoodlum, he was raised like a hoodlum, and he thinks like a hood! He didn't want his young brother Brian around to share the crown prince position with him—so he set out to get rid of him. He couldn't just have him killed, so he set out to cut him down, show him up, break his spirit, until Brian took one chance too many trying to match up to his older brother, and killed himself off."

Ian slowly nodded.

"All right!" said Tyburn. "So Kenebuck finally

succeeded. He chased Brian until the kid ran off and became a professional soldier—something Kenebuck wouldn't leave his wine, women and song long enough to shine at. And he can shine at most things he really wants to shine at, Commandant. Under that hood attitude and all those millions, he's got a good mind and a good body that he's made a hobby out of training. But, all right. So now it turns out Brian was still no good, and he took some soldiers along when he finally got around to doing what Kenebuck wanted, and getting himself killed. All right! But what can you do about it? What can anyone do about it, with all the connections, and all the money and all the law on Kenebuck's side of it? And, why should you think about doing something about it, anyway?"

"It's my duty," said Ian. He had swallowed half the whisky in his glass, absently, and now he turned the glass thoughtfully around, watching the brown liquor swirl under the forces of momentum and gravity. He looked up at Tyburn. "You know that, Lieutenant."

"Duty! Is duty that important!" demanded Tyburn. Ian gazed at him, then looked away, at the ghost-sleet beating vainly against the glass of the window that held it back in the outer dark.

"Nothing's more important than duty," said Ian, half to himself, his voice thoughtful and remote. "Mercenary troops have the right to care and protection from their own officers. When they don't get it, they're entitled to justice, so that the same thing is discouraged from happening again. That justice is a duty."

Tyburn blinked, and unexpectedly a wall seemed to go down in his mind.

"Justice for those thirty-two dead soldiers of Brian's!" he said, suddenly understanding. "That's what brought you here!"

"Yes." Ian nodded, and lifted his glass almost as if to the sleet-ghosts to drink the rest of his whisky.

"But," said Tyburn, staring at him, "You're trying to bring a civilian to justice. And Kenebuck has you out-gunned and out-maneuvered—"

The chiming of the communicator screen in one corner of the hotel room interrupted him. Ian put down his empty glass, went over to the screen and depressed a stud. His wide shoulders and back hid the screen from Tyburn, but Tyburn heard his voice.

"Yes?"

The voice of James Kenebuck sounded in the hotel room.

"Graeme—listen!"

There was a pause.

"I'm listening," said Ian, calmly.

"I'm alone now," said the voice of Kenebuck. It was tight and harsh. "My guests have gone home. I was just looking through that package of Brian's things . . ." He stopped speaking and the sentence seemed to Tyburn to dangle unfinished in the air of the hotel room. Ian let it dangle for a long moment.

"Yes?" he said, finally.

"Maybe I was a little hasty . . ." said Kenebuck. But the tone of his voice did not match the words. The tone was savage. "Why don't you come up, now that I'm alone, and we'll . . . talk about Brian, after all?"

"I'll be up," said Ian.

He snapped off the screen and turned around.

"Wait!" said Tyburn, starting up out of his chair. "You can't go up there!"

"Can't?" Ian looked at him. "I've been invited, Lieutenant."

The words were like a damp towel slapping Tyburn in the face, waking him up.

"That's right . . ." he stared at Ian. "Why? Why'd he invite you back?"

"He's had time," said Ian, "to be alone. And to look at that package of Brian's."

"But . . ." Tyburn scowled. "There was nothing important in that package. A watch, a wallet, a passport, some other papers . . . Customs gave us a list. There wasn't anything unusual there."

"Yes," said Ian. "And that's why he wants to see me again."

"But what does he want?"

"He wants me," said Ian. He met the puzzlement of Tyburn's gaze. "He was always jealous of Brian," Ian explained, almost gently. "He was afraid Brian would grow up to outdo him in things. That's why he tried to break Brian, even to kill him. But now Brian's come back to face him."

"Brian . . . ?"

"In me," said Ian. He turned toward the hotel door.

Tyburn watched him turn, then suddenly—like a man coming out of a daze, he took three hurried strides after him as Ian opened the door.

"Wait!" snapped Tyburn. "He won't be alone up there! He'll have hoods covering you through the walls. He'll definitely have traps set for you . . ."

Easily, Ian lifted the policeman's grip from his arm.

"I know," he said. And went.

Tyburn was left in the open doorway, staring after him. As Ian stepped into the elevator tube, the policeman moved. He ran for the service elevator that would take him to the police observation post above the sensors in the ceiling of Kenebuck's living room.

When Ian stepped into the foyer the second time, it was empty. He went to the door to the living room of Kenebuck's suite, found it ajar, and stepped through it. Within the room was empty, with glasses and overflowing ashtrays still on the tables; the lights had been lowered. Kenebuck rose from a chair with its back to the far, large window at the end of the room. Ian walked toward him and stopped when they were little more than an arm's length apart.

Kenebuck stood for a second, staring at him, the skin of his face tight. Then he made a short almost angry gesture with his right hand. The gesture gave away the fact that he had been drinking.

"Sit down!" he said. Ian took a comfortable chair and Kenebuck sat down in the one from which he had just risen. "Drink?" said Kenebuck. There was a decanter and glasses on the table beside and between them. Ian shook his head. Kenebuck poured part of a glass for himself.

"That package of Brian's things," he said, abruptly, the whites of his eyes glinting as he glanced up under his lids at Ian, "there was just personal stuff. Nothing else in it!"

"What else did you expect would be in it?" asked Ian, calmly.

Kenebuck's hands clenched suddenly on the glass. He stared at Ian, and then burst out into a laugh that rang a little wildly against the emptiness of the large room.

"No, no . . ." said Kenebuck, loudly. "I'm asking the questions, Graeme. I'll ask them! What made you come all the way here, to see me, anyway?"

"My duty," said Ian.

"Duty? Duty to whom—Brian?" Kenebuck looked as if he would laugh again, then thought better of it. There was the white, wild flash of his eyes again. "What was something like Brian to you? You said you didn't even like him."

"That was beside the point," said Ian, quietly. "He was one of my officers."

"One of your officers! He was my brother! That's more than being one of your officers!"

"Not," answered Ian in the same voice, "where justice is concerned."

"Justice?" Kenebuck laughed. "Justice for Brian? Is that it?"

"And for thirty-two enlisted men."

"Oh—" Kenebuck snorted laughingly. "Thirty-two men . . . those thirty-two men!" He shook his head. "I never knew your thirty-two men, Graeme, so you can't blame me for them. That was Brian's fault; him and his idea—what was the charge they tried him on? Oh, yes, that he and his thirty-two or thirty-six men could raid enemy Headquarters and come back with the enemy Commandant. Come back . . . covered with glory." Kenebuck laughed again. "But it didn't work. Not my fault."

"Brian did it," said Ian, "to show you. You were what made him do it."

"Me? Could I help it if he never could match up to me?" Kenebuck stared down at his glass and took a quick swallow from it then went back to cuddling it in his hands. He smiled a little to himself. "Never could even *catch* up to me." He looked whitely across at Ian. "I'm just a better man, Graeme. You better remember that."

Ian said nothing. Kenebuck continued to stare at him; and slowly Kenebuck's face grew more savage.

"Don't believe me, do you?" said Kenebuck, softly. "You better believe me. I'm not Brian, and I'm not bothered by Dorsais. You're here, and I'm facing you—alone."

"Alone?" said Ian. For the first time Tyburn, above the ceiling over the heads of the two men, listening and watching through hidden sensors, thought he heard a hint of emotion—contempt—in Ian's voice. Or had he imagined it?

"Alone—Well!" James Kenebuck laughed again, but a little cautiously. "I'm a civilized man, not a hick frontiersman. But I don't have to be a fool. Yes, I've got men covering you from behind the walls of the room here. I'd be stupid not to. And I've got this . . ." He whistled, and something about the size of a small dog, but made of smooth, black metal, slipped out from behind a sofa nearby and slid on an aircushion over the carpeting to their feet.

Ian looked down. It was a sort of satchel with an orifice in the top from which two metallic tentacles protruded slightly.

Ian nodded slightly.

"A medical mech," he said.

"Yes," said Kenebuck, "cued to respond to the heartbeats of anyone in the room with it. So you see, it wouldn't do you any good, even if you somehow knew where all my guards were and beat them to the draw. Even if you killed me, this could get to me in time to keep it from being permanent. So, I'm unkillable. Give up!" He laughed and kicked at the mech. "Get back," he said to it. It slid back behind the sofa.

"So you see . . ." he said. "Just sensible precautions. There's no trick to it. You're a military man— and what's that mean? Superior strength. Superior tactics. That's all. So I outpower your strength, out-number you, make your tactics useless—and what are you? Nothing." He put his glass carefully aside on the table with the decanter. "But I'm not Brian. I'm not afraid of you. I could do without these things if I wanted to."

Ian sat watching him. On the floor above, Tyburn had stiffened.

"Could you?" asked Ian.

Kenebuck stared at him. The white face of the millionaire contorted. Blood surged up into it, darkening it. His eyes flashed whitely.

"What're you trying to do—test me?" he shouted

suddenly. He jumped to his feet and stood over Ian, waving his arms furiously. It was, recognized Tyburn overhead, the calculated, self-induced hysterical rage of the hoodlum world. But how would Ian Graeme below know that? Suddenly, Kenebuck was screaming. "You want to try me out? You think I won't face you? You think I'll back down like that brother of mine, that . . ." he broke into a flood of obscenity in which the name of Brian was freely mixed. Abruptly, he whirled about to the walls of the room, yelling at them. "Get out of there! All right, out! Do you hear me? All of you! Out—"

Panels slid back, bookcases swung aside and four men stepped into the room. Three were those who had been in the foyer earlier when Ian had entered for the first time. The other was of the same type.

"Out!" screamed Kenebuck at them. "Everybody out. Outside, and lock the door behind you. I'll show this Dorsai, this . . ." almost foaming at the mouth, he lapsed into obscenity again.

Overhead, above the ceiling, Tyburn found himself gripping the edge of the table below the observation screen so hard his fingers ached.

"It's a trick!" he muttered between his teeth to the unhearing Ian. "He planned it this way! Can't you see that?"

"Graeme armed?" inquired the police sensor technician at Tyburn's right. Tyburn jerked his head around momentarily to stare at the technician.

"No," said Tyburn. "Why?"

"Kenebuck is." The technician reached over and

tapped the screen, just below the left shoulder of Kenebuck's jacket image. "Slug-thrower."

Tyburn made a fist of his aching right fingers and softly pounded the table before the screen in frustration.

"All right!" Kenebuck was shouting below, turning back to the still-seated form of Ian, and spreading his arms wide. "Now's your chance. Jump me! The door's locked. You think there's anyone else near to help me? Look!" He turned and took five steps to the wide, knee-high to ceiling window behind him, punched the control button and watched as it swung wide. A few of the whirling sleet-ghosts outside drove from out of ninety stories of vacancy, into the opening—and fell dead in little drops of moisture on the windowsill as the automatic weather shield behind the glass blocked them out.

He stalked back to Ian, who had neither moved nor changed expression through all this. Slowly, Kenebuck sank back down into his chair, his back to the night, the blocked-out cold and the sleet.

"What's the matter?" he asked, slowly, acidly. "You don't do anything? Maybe *you* don't have the nerve, Graeme?"

"We were talking about Brian," said Ian.

"Yes, Brian . . ." Kenebuck said, quite slowly. "He had a big head. He wanted to be like me, but no matter how he tried—how I tried to help him—he couldn't make it." He stared at Ian. "That's just the way, he never could make it—the way he decided to go into enemy lines when there wasn't a chance in the world. That's the way he was—a loser."

"With help," said Ian.

"What? What's that you're saying?" Kenebuck jerked upright in his chair.

"You helped him lose," Ian's voice was matter of fact. "From the time he was a young boy, you built him up to want to be like you—to take long chances and win. Only your chances were always safe bets, and his were as unsafe as you could make them."

Kenebuck drew in an audible, hissing breath.

"You've got a big mouth, Graeme!" he said, in a low, slow voice.

"You wanted," said Ian, almost conversationally, "to have him kill himself off. But he never quite did. And each time he came back for more, because he had it stuck into his mind, carved into his mind, that he wanted to impress you—even though by the time he was grown, he saw what you were up to. He knew, but he still wanted to make you admit that he wasn't a loser. You'd twisted him that way while he was growing up, and that was the way he grew."

"Go on," hissed Kenebuck. "Go on, big mouth."

"So, he went off-Earth and became a professional soldier," went on Ian, steadily and calmly. "Not because he was drafted like someone from Newton or a born professional from the Dorsai, or hungry like one of the ex-miners from Coby. But to show you you were wrong about him. He found one place where you couldn't compete with him, and he must have started writing back to you to tell you about it—half rubbing it in, half asking for the pat on the back you never gave him."

Kenebuck sat in the chair and breathed. His eyes were all one glitter.

"But you didn't answer his letters," said Ian. "I suppose you thought that'd make him desperate enough to finally do something fatal. But he didn't. Instead he succeeded. He went up through the ranks. Finally, he got his commission and made Force-Leader, and you began to be worried. It wouldn't be long, if he kept on going up, before he'd be above the field officer grades, and out of most of the actual fighting."

Kenebuck sat perfectly still, a little leaning forward. He looked almost as if he were praying, or putting all the force of his mind to willing that Ian finish what he had started to say.

"And so," said Ian, "on his twenty-third birthday—which was the day before the night on which he led his men against orders into the enemy area—you saw that he got this birthday card . . ." He reached into a side pocket of his civilian jacket and took out a white, folded card that showed signs of having been savagely crumpled but was now smoothed out again. Ian opened it and laid it beside the decanter on the table between their chairs, the sketch and legend facing Kenebuck. Kenebuck's eyes dropped to look at it.

The sketch was a crude outline of a rabbit, with a combat rifle and battle helmet discarded at its feet, engaged in painting a broad yellow stripe down the center of its own back. Underneath this picture was printed in block letters, the question—"WHY FIGHT IT?"

Kenebuck's face slowly rose from the sketch to face Ian, and the millionaire's mouth stretched at the corners, and went on stretching into a ghastly version of a smile.

"Was that all . . . ?" whispered Kenebuck.

"Not all," said Ian. "Along with it, glued to the paper by the rabbit, there was this—"

He reached almost casually into his pocket.

"No, you don't!" screamed Kenebuck triumphantly. Suddenly he was on his feet, jumping behind his chair, backing away toward the darkness of the window behind him. He reached into his jacket and his hand came out holding the slug-thrower, which cracked loudly in the room. Ian had not moved, and his body jerked to the heavy impact of the slug.

Suddenly, Ian had come to life. Incredibly, after being hammered by a slug, the shock of which should have immobilized an ordinary man, Ian was out of the chair on his feet and moving forward. Kenebuck screamed again—this time with pure terror—and began to back away, firing as he went.

"Die, you—! Die!" he screamed. But the towering Dorsai figure came on. Twice it was hit and spun clear around by the heavy slugs, but like a football fullback shaking off the assaults of tacklers, it plunged on, with great strides narrowing the distance between it and the retreating Kenebuck.

Screaming finally, Kenebuck came up with the back of his knees against the low sill of the open window. For a second his face distorted itself out of all human shape in a grimace of its terror. He looked, to right and to left, but there was no place left to run. He had been pulling the trigger of his slugthrower all this time, but now the firing pin clicked at last upon an empty chamber. Gibbering, he threw the weapon at Ian, and it flew wide of the driving figure of the Dorsai, now almost upon him, great hands outstretched.

Kenebuck jerked his head away from what was rushing toward him. Then, with a howl like a beaten dog, he turned and flung himself through the window before those hands could touch him, into ninety-odd stories of unsupported space. And his howl carried away down into silence.

Ian halted. For a second he stood before the window, his right hand still clenched about whatever it was he had pulled from his pocket. Then, like a toppling tree, he fell.

—As Tyburn and the technician with him finished burning through the ceiling above and came dropping through the charred opening into the room. They almost landed on the small object that had come rolling from Ian's now-lax hand. An object that was really two objects glued together. A small paintbrush and a transparent tube of glaring yellow paint.

"I hope you realize, though," said Tyburn, two weeks later on an icy, bright December day as he and the recovered Ian stood just inside the Terminal waiting for the boarding signal from the spaceliner about to take off for the Sirian worlds, "what a chance you took with Kenebuck. It was just luck it worked out for you the way it did."

"No," said Ian. He was as apparently emotionless as ever; a little more gaunt from his stay in the Manhattan hospital, but he had mended with the swiftness of his Dorsai constitution. "There was no luck. It all happened the way I planned it."

Tyburn gazed in astonishment.

"Why . . ." he said, "if Kenebuck hadn't had to send his hoods out of the room to make it seem necessary for him to shoot you himself when you put your hand into your pocket that second time—or if you hadn't had the card in the first place—" He broke off, suddenly thoughtful. "You mean . . . ?" he stared at Ian. "Having the card, you planned to have Kenebuck get you alone . . . ?"

"It was a form of personal combat," said Ian. "And personal combat is my business. You assumed that Kenebuck was strongly entrenched, facing my attack. But it was the other way around."

"But you had to come to him—"

"I had to appear to come to him," said Ian, almost coldly. "Otherwise he wouldn't have believed that he had to kill me—before I killed him. By his decision to kill me, he put himself in the attacking position."

"But he had all the advantages!" said Tyburn, his head whirling. "You had to fight on his ground, here where he was strong . . ."

"No," said Ian. "You're confusing the attack position with the defensive one. By coming here, I put Kenebuck in the position of finding out whether I actually had the birthday card, and the knowledge of why Brian had gone against orders into enemy territory that night. Kenebuck planned to have his men in the foyer shake me down for the card—but they lost their nerve."

"I remember," murmured Tyburn.

"Then, when I handed him the package, he was sure the card was in it. But it wasn't," went on Ian. "He saw his only choice was to give me a situation where I might feel it was safe to admit having the card and the knowledge. He had to know about that, because Brian had called his bluff by going out and risking his neck after getting the card. The fact Brian was tried and executed later made no difference to Kenebuck. That was a matter of law—something apart from hoodlum guts, or lack of guts. If no one knew that Brian was braver than his older brother, that was all right; but if I knew, he could only save face under his own standards by killing me."

"He almost did," said Tyburn. "Any one of those slugs—"

"There was the medical mech," said Ian, calmly. "A man like Kenebuck would be bound to have something like that around to play safe—just as he would be bound to set an amateur's trap." The boarding horn of the spaceliner sounded. Ian picked up his luggage bag. "Good-by," he said, offering his hand to Tyburn.

"Good-by . . ." he muttered. "So you were just going along with Kenebuck's trap, all of it. I can't believe it . . ." He released Ian's hand and watched as the big man swung around and took the first two strides away toward the bulk of the ship shining in the winter sunlight. Then, suddenly, the numbness broke clear from Tyburn's mind. He ran after Ian and caught at his arm. Ian stopped and swung half-around, frowning slightly.

"I can't believe it!" cried Tyburn. "You mean you went up there, *knowing* Kenebuck was going to pump you full of slugs and maybe kill you—all just to square things for thirty-two enlisted soldiers under the command of a man you didn't even like? I don't believe it—you can't be that cold-blooded! I don't care how much of a man of the military you are!"

Ian looked down at him. And it seemed to Tyburn that the Dorsai face had gone away from him, somehow become as remote and stony as a face carved high up on some icy mountain's top.

"But I'm not just a man of the military," Ian said. "That was the mistake Kenebuck made, too. That was why he thought that stripped of military elements, I'd be easy to kill."

Tyburn, looking at him, felt a chill run down his spine as icy as wind off a glacier.

"Then, in heaven's name," cried Tyburn. "What are you?"

Ian looked from his far distance down into Tyburn's eyes and the sadness rang as clear in his voice finally, as iron-shod heels on barren rock.

"I am a man of war," said Ian, softly.

With that, he turned and went on; and Tyburn saw him black against the winter-bright sky, looming over all the other departing passengers, on his way to board the spaceship.

A CHILDE CYCLE CONCORDANCE *(Excerpts)*

by

David W. Wixon

INTRODUCTION ◼

Even long-time readers of Gordon R. Dickson's Childe Cycle stories may be surprised to learn that Dickson has been writing those tales for over thirty years. By now, well over a million words of the collection have been published. (Casual readers should be advised that the works popularly known as the "Dorsai stories" are only a part of the Childe Cycle itself.)

During all those years and all those stories, Dickson put an immense effort into developing his work and the "universe" from which it is drawn. Utilizing a large library of painstakingly accumulated research volumes, as well as the skills of a number of generously inclined scientists, historians and researchers, the author has created in his head the image of a massive civilization, extending over a thousand years of time.

Dickson unfailingly offers readers an immense amount of detailed information that provides the realistic background for his tales. And much of that detail has never been systematically put down on paper—it exists only within the author's mind.

Dickson has himself admitted that at times he has misplaced particular details of his Cycle. It should not be a surprise to anyone if his readers, too, have trouble in remembering clearly a lot of the facts. . . .

For that reason, I have put together the following information that readers may choose to think of as a kind of encyclopedic guide to major players, places, and ideas in that portion of the Childe Cycle thus far published.

While much of this material is simply a gathering of information that Dickson has previously spread throughout his Cycle stories, some of it will be new to even the most ardent readers, because it has never before been put into print.

This can be done now because Gordie, in his normal kindly fashion, allowed me to "pump" him for information, for details that he had long ago designed into his Cycle but had never before gotten around to actually *telling* anyone. I thank him for his graciousness to me.

And I will advise the reader that there is a great deal yet remaining inside the author's head that did not make it even into *this* work. We had to stop somewhere. . . .

—David W. Wixon
21 November 1992

THE STARS

During the events chronicled in the Childe Cycle, the human race occupied a total of sixteen worlds, located in eight solar systems. One of those systems was that of Sol, which included humankind's original home planet, Earth.

The other seven solar systems—called "Younger" in the sense that the race was new to them, and they to the race—were originally pioneered by robot probes sent out from Earth during the twenty-first century. Those probes worked in conjunction with the researches of Operation Springboard, which developed the phase-shift technology that made interstellar travel possible.

During this era, the newly developed phase-shift technology was extremely dangerous to humans—which is why the first probes were robotic. But those probes enabled Earth's scientists to locate the planets of those solar systems, survey them, and take the initial steps that would lead to the terraforming of those worlds—that is, the transformation of those worlds into places habitable by human beings.

Of course probes went to solar systems other than those listed here. But human efforts were soon concentrated on the worlds that seemed most likely to be useful to humans. . . .

ON LOCATING A STAR IN EARTH'S SKY

Previously, stars were located on sky maps by means of the constellation in which they seemed, to human eyes, to lie. The concept of constellations was organized by many cultures on Earth, by people who thought they saw patterns, or pictures, in the night sky. Later astronomers have used these patterns and created more of them, so as to fill in all of the sky. There are eighty-eight standard constellations.

Constellations are not actually outlines of figures, but are simply arbitrary designations of an area to be seen in Earth's sky. The stars within a constellation usually have no real connection with each other, except that they appear from Earth to be in the same portion of the sky. If one moves some distance away from Earth, the skies will look very different and the constellation maps will become less useful.

Early astronomers attempted to name each star in the sky by order of its apparent brightness within its particular constellation. Using the Greek alphabet in order, they designated Sirius, for instance, as Alpha Canis Major, the brightest star in its constellation ("the big dog"). Similarly, the star Altair is also called Alpha Aquila, and one of the dimmer stars in the constellation Cetus is called Tau Ceti or Tau Cetus.

Early peoples long ago gave particular names to the brightest stars in their night sky, which is why a star such as Sirius has more than one name. Dimmer stars were less apt to be specially named, which is why they are now referred to by their constellation designation only—as Epsilon Eridanus, for instance.

This constellation system has been to some extent replaced by a system of coordinates, using imaginary lines in the sky similar to the lines of latitude and longitude used on maps of Earth itself. In this system, a star's declination refers to its distance north or south of the celestial equator, measured in degrees from zero to ninety, and those in turn subdivided into minutes and seconds of arc (often rounded off to the nearest minute).

In similar fashion, right ascension, measured in hours from zero to twenty-four, begins at the First Point of Aries and proceeds eastward. These hour lines, which are spaced fifteen degrees apart at the celestial equator, converge toward the north and south poles. Hours are divided into minutes and seconds, the seconds sometimes rounded out as tenths of minutes.

Coordinates are read in this order: Right Ascension/direction/declination. Thus, Arcturus would be found at 14134n1927—read as right ascension 14 hours, 13.4 minutes, declination north 19° 27′.

The distance of a star from Earth and its sun, Sol, is measured in light years—the distance light travels in one year, approximately 5,872,000,000,000 miles.

ALPHA CENTAURI

Also known as Rigel Kentaurus, the name actually refers to a triple-star system that shines brightly in the sky of the southern hemisphere of Old Earth, at position 14362s6038. The third-brightest star in Earth's sky, it is also the closest to Earth, at a distance of 4.34 light years.

Two of the system's stars orbit each other during a period of about eighty Standard Years, the distance between them varying between 1.02 and 4 billion miles.

Alpha Centauri A is of spectral type G_2, a yellow main-sequence star very nearly a twin to Sol in size and color. Its companion, Alpha Centauri B, is a slightly larger star of spectral type K_1; it is orange in color and may be variable in its brightness.

The third star in the system is known as Proxima Centauri, and it orbits the other two stars at a distance of about .17 light year. It takes its name from the fact that it is closer to Earth than the rest of the system.

Proxima Centauri is of spectral type M_5, and is a small, cool, red star, very dim, and one of the least massive stars known. It is a "flare star," and its brightness seems to vary at unpredictable intervals. It is orbited by asteroids and several small, bare planets.

Both Alpha Centauri A and B have several planets orbiting them. B's family consists of two gas giants and a lot of bare rocks—perhaps the remains of proto-planets pulled apart by the tidal strains of the system—as well as the inhabited planet, Newton.

Alpha Centauri A's planetary family includes one gas giant, several small planets, many asteroids, and one terraformed planet, Cassida.

ALTAIR

Also known as Alpha Aquila, Altair is the twelfth-brightest star seen in the sky of Old Earth. Its position in Earth's sky is 19483n0844.

Altair is currently located approximately sixteen light years from Earth. It is an A_7 spectral type, which means that it is a white main-sequence star, similar to Sirius and Fomalhaut, with a surface temperature near 10,000°K.

The star is about 1.5 times the size of Sol, and about nine times brighter. Altair rotates very rapidly upon its axis and so has the shape of a flattened ellipsoid, with an equatorial diameter nearly twice that of the polar diameter.

Altair has a modest planetary family, consisting mainly of two distant, cold gas giants, several smaller, lifeless lumps of rock, and Dunnin's World.

EPSILON ERIDANUS

Located only 10.8 light years from Earth, this K_2 star is nearly the size of Sol, but much less luminous. It is orange in color, but through some atmospheres will seem bright yellow. In Earth's sky, the star is located at 03306s0938.

E. Eridanus has a small planetary family that includes the terraformed planets Harmony and Association—which are very close in to their primary—and a super-large gas giant, much farther out, whose presence may explain certain eccentricities in the orbits of the lesser planets.

■ *Gordon R. Dickson*

FOMALHAUT

Also known as Alpha Pisces Austrinus, this star seems from Earth to lie in a fairly empty region of the sky, at 22549s2953, and was sometimes referred to as "The Solitary One." Located twenty-three light years from Earth, Fomalhaut is a main-sequence star of spectral type A_3, twice the diameter of Sol and fourteen times more luminous. It is a white star similar to Sirius, hot and bright.

Fomalhaut has a small planetary family that includes the planet known as the Dorsai.

There is an orange dwarf star of the K_5 type located about one light year from Fomalhaut. It is small and dim and has negligible effects on the planets circling the larger star.

PROCYON

Also known as Alpha Canis Minor, Procyon is located at 07367n0521 in Earth's sky and is Earth's eighth-brightest star. It is also nearby, at a distance of only 11.3 light years. The star is of type F_5, somewhat hotter and brighter than Sol and a bit more than twice the diameter, with a yellow-white color.

This star is more accurately designated as Procyon A, because it is accompanied by a companion, Procyon B. The latter is a white dwarf, small but very massive, that at times approaches close enough to the inhabited worlds to be bright in the sky.

The Procyon system has the closest group of habitable planets ever found. The terraformed planets

Mara, Kultis and Ste. Marie, in that order, circle Procyon A: Next in distance is Zombri, followed by Coby. The system also includes several lesser planets and many asteroids and comets.

SIRIUS

The brightest star in the sky of Old Earth, as well as the fifth-nearest, Sirius was a natural target of the earliest explorations from Earth. Also known as Alpha Canis Major, it is located at 06430s1639 in Earth's sky and is about 8.7 light years from Sol.

The star has long figured prominently in Earth's astronomy and mythology, and modern authorities vary as to whether its name should be translated as "The Sparkling One," "The Scorching One," "Dog Star" or "Nile Star." Because the star is fast-moving, its apparent location (to Earth eyes) has changed noticeably through the course of human history.

Sirius is an A_1 spectral-type main-sequence star, extremely luminous, with a surface temperature of approximately 10,000°K. The star is bright—about twenty-three times the luminosity of Sol—and is slightly less than twice the size of Sol.

Sirius is now brilliant white in color, with a definite tinge of blue, but there is some controversy, since many ancient commentators saw the star as *red* in color.

Sirius has a faint, white dwarf companion, which is thought to be extremely hot. This has led some scientists to speculate that this companion—known as Sirius B (the previously discussed star is Sirius A)—may have been a red giant as recently as two thousand years ago. While this theory would explain early reports, it does not match current theories of stellar evolution.

Because Sirius B is faint and close to bright Sirius A, observation is inhibited. Its mass is close to that of Sol, but it is of very low luminosity, with a diameter only one four-hundredth that of Sol, which means that the star is extremely dense. It is probably of spectral type A_5.

Sometimes known as "The Pup"—a reference to its companion's nickname of "Dog Star"—the dwarf has been reported by some observers to be itself a double star, which, if true, would make Sirius a three-star system.

Upon exploration in the late twenty-first century, these latter reports were proven incorrect. Some have speculated that those observations mistook one of the system's three gas giants for an extra star.

Since Sirius A has almost 2.5 times the mass of B, the former is the center of their system, but the presence of the massive "Pup" with its eccentric orbit—varying from 1.5 to 4 billion miles from A—has a strong effect on the remainder of the system.

The Sirian system has a large and varied planetary family, including several asteroid belts, a vast cometary cloud, gas giants and a number of smaller inner planets.

The planet nearest Sirius A is a Mercury-like baked rock. Next out is a small planet called Oriente, and then the terraformed planets Freiland and New Earth. Inhabitants of these planets have a variety of uncomplimentary names for the white dwarf that shares their system.

SOL

Also known as "The Sun," this is the star of Old Earth and humanity's origin. Sol is approximately 865,000 miles (1,400,000 km) in diameter, with a mass of about 330,000 Earths. It is a G_2 star, a yellow dwarf from the middle of the main sequence of the Hertzsprung-Russell diagram, with a surface temperature of about 5800°K.

Sol is accompanied by nine major planets and a large number of lesser bodies.

TAU CETI

Located in the sky of Old Earth at position 01417s1612, Tau Ceti is near to Sol, at about 11.8 light years' distance, but it is dim. It is a Sol-like star of spectral type G_8, slightly smaller in size that Sol and much less bright. Yellow in color, its surface temperature is about 6000°K.

The star has six planets, of which only one—Ceta—has been terraformed.

THE WORLDS

There are sixteen worlds inhabited by humankind in the Childe Cycle; they are listed in the following entries.

In casual conversation, people often refer to the "sixteen worlds" in the same manner that Earth people say "the whole world." But at times, you may hear a reference to "thirteen" or "fourteen" worlds.

People speaking of "the thirteen Younger Worlds" are in fact separating the earliest-settled planets—Earth, Mars and Venus—from the remainder of the inhabited worlds, which of course number thirteen.

Those who refer to the "fourteen worlds" are unconsciously remembering that two human societies—the Exotics and the Friendlies—each inhabit two planets and so are counting those societies as *one* "world" each, thus achieving a total count of fourteen "worlds."

ASSOCIATION

One of two inhabited planets in the system of Epsilon Eridanus, Association, like its neighbor Harmony, is a metal-poor world. It lacks most natural resources, in fact, and so its people, descendants of the original religious colonists, generally remain in virtual poverty while trying to farm the poor soil with homemade tools.

Association orbits close to its primary and is strongly inclined to the plane of its ecliptic. Its year is very short—about eighty Standard Days—and features an extremely hot summer of a few weeks' duration, followed by a longer, rainy winter. On most of the planet, farmers raise their crops during the winter; the entire population tries to stay undercover during the summer.

The preponderance of the planet's land mass lies in the temperate zones. The poles have little land, and that is usually under sheets of ice or standing water, depending on the season.

Association had its own native ecological system before being terraformed. Remnants survive, but most plants are variforms: genetically altered Earth plants such as trees, grasses and grains. Most Earth-descended animals do not seem to breed well on the planet, for reasons not yet understood. Rabbits do well, and the planet suffers from a virtual plague of them. Some farmers raise goats, but this animal, too, seldom breeds true and most have to be imported from Earth in the form of very expensive embryos.

The planet's capital is Ecumeny, site of the legislature, the Chamber of Speakers, but in interstellar affairs, both Friendly worlds act as a unit.

CASSIDA

The planet named Cassida happens to lie in the same solar system as the planet Newton; this fact has determined nearly all of human existence on Cassida.

The planet is in the Alpha Centauri system, which is a triple-star system near to Earth. Unlike the other inhabited planet in the system (Newton), Cassida orbits the star known as Alpha Centauri A, a Sol-like yellow star.

Cassida is slightly smaller than Earth and is fairly wealthy. In part, this is because the planet, unlike many of the Younger Worlds, has a modest supply of metal resources.

■ *Gordon R. Dickson*

Due to difficulty in the terraforming process, Cassida was settled later than its neighbor, Newton. And while Cassida's pioneering settlers were struggling to open up the planet, Newton had already begun the process of specialization that would ultimately make it the scientific research capital of human space.

Unable to compete with Newton, the people of Cassida began to cooperate with their neighbors. Blessed with a small amount of various metals and plentiful supplies of energy, the Cassidans became skilled at turning Newton's scientific discoveries into profitable products; in short, they became the engineers and marketing directors who helped make both themselves and the Newtonians rich. Cassida also trains skillful technicians.

Newton has thus had a strong hand in the formation of Cassidan society, which in turn has a tendency to react to Newton as to a senior partner and a model to be followed. Thus Cassida, after its free-spirited pioneering days, has revamped its loose, open ways to reflect the Newtonian view that people are just one more resource of a society.

Perhaps as a result, the Cassidan culture began to show signs of dysfunction; by the mid-twenty-fourth century, there had developed a substantial history of apparently sane citizens suddenly running amok, killing others until they were deterred or themselves slain.

CETA

The planet called Ceta takes its name from its sun, the star designated Tau Ceti. Ceta is the youngest world in terms of its settlement by humans.

The star Tau Ceti, being relatively close to Earth and very similar to Earth's sun, was a natural early target for human exploration. The first robot exploratory craft found the Tau Ceti system to have a number of planets, of which only one could possibly be eventually habitable. The planet has no moon.

That planet was the largest ever found capable of terraforming; it lay well within a temperate climatic range and possessed several large land masses separated by modest-sized but deep oceans. However, the atmosphere was largely made up of inert gases, and no life had developed on the planet. Although larger than Earth, the planet's gravity was weaker.

This presented a unique terraforming problem, and while the problem was being solved, human settlement of the other Younger Worlds proceeded.

When the planet was opened to human settlement in the second half of the twenty-second century, its vast land masses and varied terrain attracted a wide variety of settlers. A large number of groups came, searched out the choicest lands and settled in. The planet lacked metal supplies, but its congenial climates allowed most colonies to prosper quickly, and the variety of terrains and climates meant that colonies tended to produce a surplus of different items.

Inter-colony trade flourished early despite a certain amount of friction, and Cetan expertise in commer-

cial affairs blossomed. This reputation was over-
stated during the second half of the twenty-third century, when the ingenious manipulations of the
schemer called Prince William of Ceta led the worlds
to give Cetans the reputation of master entrepreneurs.
But in fact, the vast majority of the planet's residents
are farmers and laborers. Earth-descended cattle
thrive on Ceta.

The planet lost much of that reputation after William's arrest by Donal Graeme, near the end of the
century. Since that time, the planet has been relatively quiet in interstellar affairs. Its large continents
are still partly unexplored and unsettled, and pioneering settlers continue to arrive.

The planet has a relatively small number of cities
for its size; those cities tend to be densely populated
by poorly educated, low-income people who have
not been able to succeed elsewhere on the planet.
The situation has kept politics in ferment on local
levels.

Ceta has no planet-wide government as such. Governmental functions remain in the hands of the large
number of small states, which vary widely in form
and function. Even in the days of Prince William's
ascendancy, governance was in fact based on economic pressures that bent those states to the prince's
will.

The planet's capital, also named Ceta, exists only
for the purpose of providing liaison between the
other human worlds and Ceta's many nations. There
are no true government functions, only information
and communications services.

COBY

Coby is the outermost of the inhabited worlds of the Procyon system; however, its position has no significance to its inhabitants, who live underground. The planet is probably impossible to terraform, its surface being a nearly airless rock-and-dust desert. Its people need to create their very air and water out of crustal chemicals.

The reason people go through such effort to live in Coby can be found in the planet's makeup; it has a large, accessible supply of a wide variety of metals. Astrophysicists surmise that the planet may in fact be a wanderer from outside the Procyon system—a minority even suggest a more esoteric origin in a nova—primarily because its makeup is so different from other bodies in the system.

The planet was largely ignored when first discovered, simply because it took a while for people to realize that the other new planets they had discovered were generally very short of metals. Indeed, the societies developing on most of those new worlds were starved for metals, without which they could not survive as viable cultures.

That makes Coby the only one of the Younger Worlds that exports in quantity anything besides technological items and brainpower.

Settlement began as a series of mines that dug themselves into the planet and eventually were connected by tunnels. There was no government, and power rested in the companies owning the mines. Those companies had nearly absolute domain over the miners they signed to contracts. Conditions were harsh, the miners the sweepings of the other worlds—for no one but the desperate would work there in the early years. The companies never bothered with importing modern mining equipment, finding it cheaper to use up men and women in brutal manual labor.

As the mines continued to expand, Coby society became increasingly anarchic, until eventually interstellar public opinion led the mining companies to form a Planetary Consortium of Companies, which took on quasi-governmental functions. At the same time, there was a growing need for non-mining personnel, and a varied society began to develop, with some slight alleviation of the harshest conditions.

Among the features unique to Coby are gigantic underground airlocks; spaceships coming to the planet do not usually park in orbit, but settle into huge cradles, where they are either loaded with the metals they will freight out or undergo repairs. Coby is, of course, able to replace fabricated metal fittings more cheaply than any other world.

Coby has one small moon, but its people never see it.

THE DORSAI (planet)

Located in orbit about Fomalhaut, the Dorsai is the most distant from Earth of the human-settled worlds. It was, accordingly, the last to be reached by the automated probes sent out from Earth.

By the time the planet had been surveyed, the

process of terraforming the planets reached earlier was well under way. Financial support for and political interest in the expensive process was waning on Earth, but the newfound planet actually required only a small amount of work—generally in the form of seeding the planet with genetically engineered Earth-descended life forms.

The Dorsai was a planet of oceans dotted with islands. Somewhat smaller than Earth, the planet's land masses totaled an area less than half that of Earth's land surface. The Dorsai has no land deserving of the term "continent" (although the largest island is named South Continent, it was so designated as a kind of joke).

The planet is thought to be in a warm stage of its geological cycles; its ice caps are shrunken and its seas are higher than they apparently were in past geological eras. Those seas contain the only native animal life: herbivorous marine life forms, inedible by man.

Fomalhaut is a large, hot sun, and the Dorsai, orbiting in its habitable zone, is far out from its primary; the planet's year is thus longer than the Interstellar Standard Year, based on Earth's year. And even in this "warm" geological era, the planet is cold, difficult to make a living on.

The Dorsai is badly lacking in metals, and dietary supplements are necessary for human health. There are petroleum fields, generally out in shallow seabeds. Farmlands are scanty and of low fertility; much of the land that thrusts above sea level is mountainous and stony, the small amount of soil between rocks suitable only for pasturage.

The planet had developed some plant life of its own—on land, mostly in the form of grasses, bushes and some treelike forms. Earth plants such as grasses and conifers have flourished and almost shouldered aside the native forms. Earth flowers, insects and some birds have been successfully adapted to the planet, along with larger life forms such as rabbits, foxes, goats and sheep. The Dorsai, for reasons not at all clear to biologists, is one of the few Younger Worlds upon which horses can flourish.

At sea, Earth-descended creatures, genetically engineered ("variformed") to fit the planet, have established a thriving ecology that coexists successfully with the incompatible native ecology. Dorsai fisheries provide the largest protein source in the Dorsai diet. And the sea ecology also includes a variety of sea mammals, amphibians, and birds such as gulls, puffins, hawks and eagles.

Because others of the Younger Worlds had been settled well before the Dorsai, and because the planet was easily habitable, people were coming to the Dorsai before the terraforming process had been officially completed. Generally, they were people who were not comfortable, or not wanted, on the other worlds. None bought licenses to settle; they simply "squatted."

In many cases, they were mercenary soldiers who, having fought in some inter-colony brush war on one of the new worlds, had been paid off and then told to go away (until they were needed again). On this new

frontier world, without government or other authority, they found that they could, in effect, take a vaca-
tion, camping in the mountains or on the seashore,
before leaving the planet to return to the wars.

Eventually, some of them made the planet—only
now beginning to be referred to with a name—their
permanent headquarters, setting up homes and families alongside the few non-soldier pioneers.

Most of these mercenary soldiers were only mini-
mally skilled, providing nothing more than cannon
fodder for the wars. Many of those who went out to
war never came back; those who did had been paid
poorly. And those who died were generally replaced
by new mercenaries, drawn from the less-desirable
elements of many societies.

For years, the more prosperous settlers were
plagued by the depredations of loosely formed gangs
of unemployed mercenaries who, camping in squalor
in the mountains, emerged periodically to raid and
loot. Eventually, the settlers turned on them in
vigilante-like action, wiping out some gangs in a virtual war and running the rest of them off the planet.
Much of this action was in fact taken by those who
could not leave the planet to earn money at war:
wives and widows, children and old men. These people took many casualties, but they took, also, the
planet.

Most of the Younger Worlds were settled by organized groups who paid licensing fees to the
megacorporations that had terraformed the planets.
As part of their services, the corporations had
stocked the worlds with some rudimentary roads,

power stations, landing pads, town sites and libraries.

The Dorsai, settled so informally, had none of this, nor any organized space travel service. Dorsai settlers, on a world already lacking many natural resources, had to provide and pay for their own economic infrastructure, as well as import most of the necessities of life. Indeed, they even had to finance the continued seeding of Earth life forms about the planet, and many early Dorsai scraped and saved for years to import a horse embryo or a batch of seedlings.

It was a bitter life for a planet that needed much and had nothing to sell off-planet but the lives of its sons. The Dorsai people came to see themselves as a single people, separate from others, and they began to develop an ethic of responsibility, and of the willingness to do what had to be done, no matter the cost.

For several generations, Dorsai soldiers had no great reputation between the stars. Off-worlders were unwilling to employ more than small groups of them as units of larger forces; pay remained poor and recognition negligible. Then Cletus Grahame immigrated to the Dorsai.

Grahame, armed with his own genius and the financial backing of the Exotics, persuaded some influential Dorsai leaders to join him in a retraining program. The planet still had no government, but as Grahame followed success with new success, the Dorsai, deeply appreciative of his ability to increase their income while cutting down on their casualties, committed themselves wholly to his methods.

Grahame's reputation, and that of the Dorsai, was made when the planet defeated the combined Earth forces, led by Dow deCastries, which invaded the Dorsai—while most of the fighting men were off-planet. Thereafter, Dorsai soldiers commanded premium pay; within a few generations, it began to be said that if they wished, the Dorsai could fight the forces of all the other worlds combined and win.

Probably this was untrue, if only because of numbers. During Grahame's time, the total number of Dorsai soldiers was near twenty thousand, and this represented roughly a twelfth of the total population. The planet would always remain sparsely populated, but the efficiency of Dorsai soldiery required no great numbers.

After Grahame's innovations—including his teachings on tactics and strategy—the Dorsai's increased income enabled them to import expensive items such as complete modern manufactories, advanced medical technologies and their own spacecraft.

Always, such things were done by individual Dorsai, or by groups of them. The planet has never established a central government, and the facilities at Omalu—the closest thing to a capital on the planet— function mostly as a library, and as an information and coordination center: facilities useful to the contractors who negotiate and put together the contracts for off-world soldiering.

The Dorsai has been divided into Districts—later to be called Cantons—but in practice, such have little authority over individuals and function mostly so as to express local public opinion. The Dorsai people brook no interference with their freedoms.

On this world, families—even individuals—are constantly dealing on a direct and independent basis with off-planet governments and people. No government strong enough to interfere with this tradition has been allowed to develop. The Cantons remain independent of the United Cantons and the families of the Cantons. Dorsai work together only voluntarily, on the basis of cooperation and the agreement in a contract.

Because Dorsai individuals and families deal so much with off-planet affairs, their investments to further their livelihoods have included spacecraft and spacepads. In fact, the Dorsai has an unusually high number of both—more than any other Younger World, probably more than a number of them together.

The Dorsai has a single moon, a misshapen lump of rock that at times appears to be two separate bodies—a "double" moon—as it lines up in the sky with the nearby dwarf star that the Dorsai call Nightlight.

DUNNIN'S WORLD

This fourth planet of Altair has been terraformed but even so, it remains sparsely populated and unattractive. It is poor in metals and minerals and is a dry, dusty planet. Its soil is heavily alkaline—and, for that matter, so are its small bodies of water. The planet's residents have not been able to afford to correct those conditions.

The planet was first settled in the mid-twenty-second century by underworld elements seeking a place not subject to normal planetary laws. A few oases were settled as gambling dens, and before long, the planet came under the loose rule of the Corbel, a sort of cooperative society with ties to the underworlds of a number of other planets. The society's principal purpose lay in enticing prosperous citizens of other planets to come and sample the many vices available at Dunnin's.

The Corbel eventually disintegrated, and the planet sank into a struggle for subsistence. None of the larger Earth animals has proved able to live on the planet, so the people largely survive on fish, rabbits and goats, supplemented by irrigation farming.

EARTH

Third planet of the Sol system, Earth is the original home of humanity and is often referred to by off-worlders as Old Earth in a somewhat defiant differentiation from the colony world of New Earth.

Rich and heavily populated, Earth spun off a number of colonies in the late twenty-first and early twenty-second centuries. During the latter century, tensions arose as those colonies began to struggle among themselves. The nations of Earth, roughly divided into two large alliances, often took sides in these struggles, seeking to maintain ascendancy among the stars.

After Cletus Grahame goaded Dow deCastries into the abortive invasion of the Dorsai, Earth drew back from the stars, and the colonies became independent. Old Earth, still by far the richest, most heavily populated world, turned its attention to other pursuits, including massive projects to rehabilitate desert areas and the construction of the Final Encyclopedia.

Never truly united, Earth continued to harbor literally hundreds of governmental bodies—some of which, created to handle specific problems, overlapped, such as the large Agricultural Districts and the Weather Control Authority.

Every social, religious and ethnic group continued to demand a degree of autonomy from those about it. But they usually participate willingly in the more general All-Earth participant political bodies that consider and rule on matters involving the whole planet. These bodies are often deadlocked, and so Earth is seldom an active participant in interstellar affairs.

Earth's population continues to number more than twenty times that of any other world, as well as more than that of all the other worlds combined.

FREILAND

Freiland is the third planet of Sirius and shares its system with another inhabited world, New Earth. Freiland is slightly smaller than Old Earth and is blessed with a moderate amount of metals and a plentitude of power sources. The planet has fertile land masses, and oceans that although small in size, teem with Earth-descended variform fish. Since the planet has no moon, tides are small.

The planet was first settled by groups from northern Europe on Old Earth, people often of rigid personality and strong communal feelings. Although groups from other areas later immigrated to Freiland, the society has continued to be characterized by bureaucratization of governmental as well as private organizations.

Rich and largely self-sufficient, Freiland and its people, while nonspecialized, developed a strong work ethic. Unadventurous in off-world affairs, the planet has unobtrusively become wealthier and more commercially active than even its companion under Sirius, New Earth.

While the planet seems on the surface to be prosperous, happy, well-organized and industrious, it is troubled by high rates of suicide and addictions to alcohol and various drugs. Gambling, night life and spectator sports occupy the attention of a large number of the populace, and there is increasing lack of interest in holding jobs—this last a recent development that has societal leaders worried.

HARMONY

The larger of the two inhabited planets under Epsilon Eridanus, Harmony is farther out from their sun than is its sister planet, Association. Its day is 23.16 Interstellar Standard Hours in length, and it has one moon, named The Eye of the Lord.

Harmony has several large continents, separated

by oceans. The planet had its own native ecology before being terraformed, and some native plant forms continue to exist side by side with the imported Earth-descended forms. A few of the native forms have been adapted to make them compatible with an Earthling ecology.

Horses, dogs and other large Earth life forms generally do not seem able to reproduce on Harmony, with the exception of sheep, goats and donkeys. Smaller Earth creatures have proven more resilient.

Along with its sister planet Association, Harmony is a poor place, starved for metals and possessed of thin, stony soil. Both planets were settled at the same time by the groups who came to be called the Friendlies, religious sects who, generally dirt poor, nevertheless succeeded in turning large families into a sizable population, usually divided against itself by religious arguments.

After several poverty-stricken centuries, Harmony was able to accumulate enough wealth to construct two Core Tap power stations. Originally almost devoid of technology and wealth, the planet now has a small rich class, but most of the population is still poor.

KULTIS

Kultis is an inhabited world of the Procyon system, where it orbits that star between Mara and Ste. Marie. The planet is larger than Earth, and also larger than its two neighboring worlds. Relatively close to Procyon, Kultis is a warm world—and because the angle of its axis to its orbit is small, it has a wide tropical zone.

The planet has two main continental masses, one each in the northern and southern hemispheres. Those continents are so huge that they have been arbitrarily divided into smaller "continents," much as Europe and Asia are divided on Earth. There are two moons in Kultis's sky.

Although lacking in metals and certain trace elements necessary to human diets, Kultis is an extraordinarily fertile world. After discovery, it required only a small amount of terraforming to be habitable; the main problem lay in the bioengineering of variformed Earth-descended plants that could successfully battle for space against the verdant native vegetation.

Kultis had a large and varied native ecosystem which, while lacking large animals, nonetheless filled the planet. At lower altitudes, the land was a hot, steamy jungle, the very air and water infused with varieties of plant life that gave them greenish or yellowish tinges. At higher, cooler altitudes, Earth life had easier success.

Like its sister planet Mara, Kultis was originally settled by colonies representing a variety of social and political ideas. This mix provided a fertile ground for the Earth-born struggle between the Coalition and the Alliance, but the Exotics of Bakhalla Colony managed to survive and prosper. Clever, farsighted and cooperative, the Exotics quickly came to dominate Kultis as they did Mara. Even without formal governmental bodies, the two planets now function as a powerful unit.

MARA

Part of the extraordinary string of inhabited planets for which the Procyon system is noted, Mara lies closest to the primary. The planet is slightly larger than Earth and has no moon.

Mara is quite warm, of course, but the heat of the tropical zones is moderated by nearby seas. Most of the land masses lie in the temperate zones, which, despite their name, are warmer than comparable zones on Old Earth.

Mara has only the smallest of ice caps, which are transient with the seasons. None but the lands nearest to the poles, or the highest mountains, will ever see snow.

The planet's name is that of the Buddhist Satan and was bestowed on the planet by one of the earliest colonies of Chantry Guild refugees, a group that still clung to certain of its "black-magic" beliefs. A variety of other groups also colonized the planet, which did not require a great deal of terraforming to make it habitable.

Native life forms were largely limited to plants, and those still survive on Mara, interspersed among imported Earth plants that have been "variformed"— bioengineered to suit the planet. Human and other Earth-descended life forms, of course, cannot eat native Maran life forms, except for those few that have been variformed for human use. In fact, humans require dietary supplements in any case, because the planet is severely deficient in a number of the trace elements and metals necessary for optimum human health.

As is the case with many of the Younger Worlds, most of the larger Earth animals have not been successfully adapted to Mara. Biologists do not yet fully understand the reasons for this.

Colonized in its early years by groups from many parts of Earth, representing a wide variety of social and political strains, Mara was an early theater of battle for Alliance and Coalition forces. These two Earth power blocs, through puppet colonies, struggled for control of the planet only to find themselves outflanked when the Exotics established a Core Tap power station at the North Pole.

In the wake of Cletus Grahame's defeat of Earth and Dow deCastries, Exotic control of the Core Tap and the cheap, plentiful energy it supplied, led quickly to economic domination of the planet. Cultural and philosophical conversion of the non-Exotic colonies followed peacefully over the course of the next century.

Mara now has no government in any conventionally accepted sense of the term.

MARS

Mars, fourth planet of the Sol system, lies approximately 142 million miles from its sun. Its year lasts 687 Standard Days, and its day is 24 hours, 27 minutes long. Mars is the smallest inhabited world, at slightly more than half Earth-size, and has very low gravity.

Mars is the first planet to have been colonized from Earth and the first upon which terraforming experiments were attempted. These experiments succeeded in raising the planet's temperature somewhat and in converting the planet's carbon-dioxide atmosphere, but Mars remains cold and uncomfortable, with water shortages.

Originally colonized by pioneers interested in specialized farming, the planet was largely subsidized by Earth financing for the terraforming experiments. When that support withered away, Mars became a quiet backwater of the interstellar community.

The planet has two tiny moons, Phobos and Deimos.

NEW EARTH

The fourth planet of the Sirius system, New Earth was one of the first to be reached by the drone spacecraft of Operation Springboard. Despite a dusty yellow sky and a thick hydrogen-sulphide odor in the atmosphere, the planet was quickly and easily terraformed and settled.

New Earth was pioneered by scores of groups from Earth, and the individual colonies prospered. The planet became one of the richest of the Younger Worlds, although its varied climates and cultures made for frequent inter-colony wars.

Unlike some other worlds, New Earth was never melded into one major culture but has remained a polyglot of subcultures, which form a federation for purposes of all-world affairs. The people seem to resemble Earth populations in many respects—including their wide variety—and the planet is one of the few Younger Worlds which, like Ceta, successfully raise Earth-descended cattle.

New Earth has no moon of its own; it shares the Sirian system, however, with the inhabited planet Freiland in a kind of friendly rivalry.

NEWTON

The planet Newton lies in the triple-sun solar system of Alpha Centauri, where it orbits the star known as Alpha Centauri B. Newton is a little larger than Earth, and is larger than Cassida, the other inhabited planet in the system.

Newton frequently features a cloud cover over much of its surface, which from space obscures the fact that the planet has large, green continents and small, green-tinted oceans. Newton's primary is an orange star whose light reflecting off the clouds gives the planet, seen from space, an orangish appearance.

The planet has five moons. Three of them are quite small, no more than captured asteroids; the two larger moons are the only ones that are really noticeable, either to Newtonians or to space travelers. Offworlders have been known to refer to Newton, in sour fashion, as "the orange and the two pips."

Newton was a large, rich planet with a primitive ecosystem of its own when discovered by the first robot probes of Operation Springboard from Earth. Because Alpha Centauri is the closest solar system to Earth, Newton was the first planet outside of Earth's system to be terraformed.

Because Newton was a rich planet, it attracted large numbers of settlers from many areas of Earth, as well as from Venus. Many of the immigrants were of a strong technical and scientific background; over a period of almost a century, these groups banded together under the name of Advanced Associated Communities and came to dominate all other groups on the planet.

Because of these Communities, the planet invested heavily in scientific research, quickly rivaling and then surpassing Venus as the off-Earth leader in the field. Wealth gained by licensing of its discoveries caused the planet to quickly become the richest, after Earth.

Newton is governed by scientists, the senior of whom form the planet's House of Representatives. But they comprise an unwieldy and uninterested body and leave the actual government to an executive committee, which varies in number and has at times been known by such names as the Board of Governors or the Laboratories Review Council.

Focusing on technology, Newton has historically been an ingrown society. Newtonians generally avoid outsiders when they can, leaving it to their satellite, the Cassidans, to manage business dealings. Newtonians control their society and people tightly and have a strong antipathy for the seemingly undisciplined, mystical Exotics.

ORIENTE

A minor planet of the Sirius system, Oriente is too small and too close to its sun for terraforming. It has a thin atmosphere, largely composed of carbon dioxide at a low pressure, and of course cannot sustain human life. There is very little water on the planet, and its surface is a rock desert, with occasional patches of cactus-like jungle.

The planet has occasionally played minor parts in the history of politics of the Sirian system, but it is too uncomfortable to be anything more than a platform.

SAINTE MARIE

The second smallest inhabitable planet, Ste. Marie is part of the Procyon system, along with the two Exotic planets and Coby. Originally settled mainly by immigrants from western and southern Europe, the planet is predominantly Roman Catholic in culture. It is a green, lush world, with agriculture as its main industry.

The planet is still principally rural in character, but the growth of the small cities has led to some political friction between rural and urban groups. However, Ste. Marie's politics remain generally quiet, its original democratic theocracy having faded in influence.

In interstellar affairs, Ste. Marie is almost a ward of the Exotics, the major power that shares their system. In truth, there is no official connection between the two societies, but the Exotics, always pragmatic, take whatever action necessary to keep foreign influences out of Ste. Marie's affairs. Ste. Marie does not maintain a standing army other than a two-thousand-man militia, and it never gets involved in interstellar conflicts.

VENUS

Second planet of the Sol system, Venus is the closest planet to Old Earth. It lies 67 million miles from its sun, and its year lasts 225 Standard Days.

Venus is nearly the same size as Earth, and for a long time, Earth people dreamed of creating a nearby twin of the Mother Planet. Very early in Earth's space experience, scientific stations were set up on the surface of Venus, as well as in orbit about it.

The megacorporations that would one day terraform the other Younger Worlds were not yet in existence, and so these early stations were largely funded by Earth governments. It was quickly learned that while Venusian conditions—900°F temperatures, pressures of 90 atmospheres, a rough surface, and a carbon-dioxide atmosphere with sulphuric-acid clouds but no water—made terraforming difficult, they presented a valuable laboratory for other sorts of researchers.

Scientific work, Earth financing and the dream of a reclaimed planet continued to draw people to Venus. The scientific stations grew and linked together, and the capital city, Holmstead, became a sort of boom town. To the struggling Younger Worlds, Venus presented a picture of the prosperity of a scientific juggernaut; by the second half of the twenty-third century, under the leadership of Project Blaine, the planet seemed a power in interstellar affairs.

But as the dream of terraforming Venus died, Earth withdrew her funding and her interest. It was quickly learned that the planet's prosperity had been an artificial construction. Venus soon lost its influence and reverted to being a string of half-populated research stations once again.

ZOMBRI

This tiny planet, perhaps more accurately described as an escaped moon, lies in the Procyon system, in an eccentric orbit between Ste. Marie and Coby. Zombri is not habitable, having only traces of an atmosphere. No ice and no life forms have been found. Terraforming is not currently feasible.

The planet would be of no significance at all were it not for its location, which gives it a certain strategic value in contests for control of the Procyon system. For this reason, the Exotics have always opposed any interest in the planetoid on the part of outside powers.

PEOPLE, PLACES AND CONCEPTS

BLEYS AHRENS

Like his older half brother Dahno, Bleys Ahrens was born to a woman who had rejected her Exotic heritage and become a kind of courtesan. Raised as an isolated and lonely child, Bleys was extremely intelligent, which had the effect of heightening his sense of isolation. Nevertheless, he was intelligent enough to realize that he needed to escape from his mother's control.

Like Dahno before him, Bleys managed to arrange to be sent away from his mother, and although Bleys' father was not known, Ezekiel MacLean stepped in to take responsibility for the boy and shipped him to his brother, Henry MacLean, on Association. Bleys was eleven years old.

On Association, being raised by Henry MacLean, Bleys determined to try to make himself into a Friendly, being attracted to the sense of purpose with which they lived and by the certainty they obviously felt. Meanwhile, he was being cultivated and educated by Dahno, and when Bleys failed to become a Friendly, he set himself to become as knowledgeable as he could about Dahno's business.

Even more intelligent than his older brother, Bleys soon learned all there was to know about Dahno's organization, known as the "Others." And he found in himself a use for the organization, and so began to take it over.

Desperately needing a purpose by which to guide his life, Bleys conceived of the notion that the human race had left Earth too soon and would die off if it continued on its present course. He determined that the best thing to do was to force the race to return to Earth and stay there, until at some theoretical time it would have changed enough to be able to return to space in safety. The people of Earth would be controlled; the peoples of the Younger Worlds would be left to die out by themselves.

Self-directed and immensely talented, Bleys spent years preparing himself for the mission he had invented for himself. Although he became as tall as his brother, Bleys was not as big as Dahno. But he trained himself arduously in everything from phase-shift mechanics to the martial arts. Lacking Dahno's talent for persuasion, Bleys nonetheless did his best to develop his abilities in that area. Tall, handsome and athletic, he cultivated his voice and his mind, seeking to make them able to work with his striking appearance so as to be able to capture people's attention and focus it upon himself and his message.

Denied Dahno's innate talent, Bleys used what he had, along with hard work, to become the true leader of the Others—and soon of eleven worlds waging a war against Earth.

Friendless and isolated all his life, Bleys found himself strangely intrigued by the leader of the opposition to his plans, the young Hal Mayne. Hal is the only one Bleys ever met who might be his equal.

DAHNO AHRENS

Often known simply as Dahno, or perhaps Danno, he is the ten-years-older half brother of Bleys Ahrens and, like Bleys, is the illegitimate son of an Exotic expatriate woman. It is not known who Dahno's father was, although an expatriate Friendly named Ezekiel MacLean took responsibility for the boy when his mother sent him away from her.

Dahno was an unusual child, very intelligent and at the age of twelve, as large as a grown man. He tried to run away from his mother at about that age, and so was exiled. At Ezekiel's intervention, Dahno was sent to live with Ezekiel's brother, Henry MacLean, who farmed a poor holding on the planet Association.

After a short time on the MacLean farm, Dahno moved to the planet's capital, Ecumeny. He had become a veritable giant, tall and broad, and was comparably strong. He had curly, jet-black hair over a round and merry face, and his warm smile was matched by his warm, light-baritone voice.

Dahno proved to have an immense talent; a natural ability to ingratiate himself with people. He could *charm* almost anyone, and when he set himself up in business as a kind of lobbyist, he quickly became a success and obtained a powerful influence in Association's ruling circles.

He had greater ambitions, however, that led him to take over a social group called the "Others," originally a sort of support group for people bred of more than one of the Splinter Cultures. He educated and indoctrinated them on the means to form satellite organizations on a number of the other worlds—organizations that began to gain influence on their worlds while feeding information back to Dahno.

Having set the organization in motion, Dahno nonetheless remained mainly concerned with affairs on Association itself.

Dahno also took his younger brother, Bleys, into the organization and educated him to take the role of his top assistant.

AJELA

A young Exotic woman from Mara, she was one of "Padma's children," a group of fifty exceptional Exotic children raised by the legendary Exotic thinker in a special manner. Unlike most Exotic children, these children were exposed not only to their own Exotic culture, but to elements of the Dorsai and Friendly cultures. They were given more freedom to bond emotionally to other individuals, which Exotics historically tried to avoid, and to indulge in romantic rather than logical thinking. This system was set up because Padma suspected that there had been a blind spot in Exotic thinking that had caused Exotic onto-geneticists to make several errors; it was hoped that this project might result in rearing Exotics who were able to see their way around that blind spot.

The children were thus set free to fall in love with things that most Exotic children were taught to regard as unproductive subjects. Ajela, for her part, fell in love with the story of Tam Olyn and the Final Encyclopedia, and by the time she was eleven, she had convinced everyone involved to let her come to the Encyclopedia. She worked directly with the Director of the Final Encyclopedia, Tam Olyn himself; before she was twenty, she had become his Special Assistant and was doing much of the day-to-day running of the entire installation. She had also fallen in love with Tam himself, for all that he was well over his century mark.

Ajela is fair of skin, with a round face, and blue eyes that in some lights may look green. Her hair is long and a golden blond in color, and her features are rather delicate. She is not particularly small but gives that impression. Her posture is straight, and she carries an air of firmness and decision, which to some people seems very non-Exotic. She *runs* things.

JAMETHON BLACK

A native of Harmony, from the village of Remembered-of-the-Lord, whose people are of predominantly Berber ancestry, Jamethon Black was a promising young officer in his culture's military forces when he fell in love with a young Earthwoman, Eileen Olyn. A thin, dark young man of medium height, dressed all in black, he presented a picture of a Friendly religious fanatic, which led Eileen's brother to end their relationship.

Thereafter Black became the focus of Tam Olyn's attempt to destroy the Friendly culture—an attempt that failed simply and only because of Jamethon's fidelity to his Faith. Black lost his life on Ste. Marie but by doing so, he saved his troops, his culture—and Tam Olyn himself. His life perfectly exemplified the power of his Faith.

WALTER BLUNT

An English immigrant to the United States during the twenty-first century, Blunt was nearly killed during a hunting trip. He conceived of the Alternate Forces of existence, his explanation for the mental powers he developed to save his life.

Blunt was a large, gaunt, older man, with wide shoulders. He generally walked with a cane, although it is not clear that he really needed such assistance.

Walter Blunt saw that there were massive levels of unhappiness among the people living amid Earth's burgeoning technological civilization. In response, he founded the Chantry Guild, intended to help people who were capable of it, to find their way to an understanding of the Alternate Forces.

It was Blunt's belief that mankind was caught in the grip of a technological civilization that was stifling the race and making it sick. He proclaimed that the only cure was DESTRUCT!—the violent revolution intended to destroy technological civilization. This, Blunt felt, would *force* mankind to develop in another direction, one that would make use of people's innate abilities and enable them to become godlike.

Blunt truly had tremendous powers of the paranormal variety, and he was able to help other people to develop them, too. But when he tried to use his powers to make a dead man a pawn in his war against the Super-Complex, his weapon was turned against him by an unsuspected outside power.

■ *Gordon R. Dickson*

THE CHANTRY GUILD

Established late in the twenty-first century by Walter Blunt in the United States, the Chantry Guild took its name from a medieval European institution known as a chantry. Generally speaking, a chantry was a small church or chapel—or the endowment that financed it—that had been established by some person or group seeking to have prayers regularly offered for some particular purpose, usually for the salvation of the souls of the donors.

Blunt used the term for its implication of a search for salvation, because he believed that humankind needed to be saved from the corrosive effects of the modern technologically based civilization.

Blunt's Chantry Guild became a sort of loose federation of anti-technological groups ranging from believers in "natural religion" through political anarchists to satanists and mentalists. Blunt's loudly proclaimed message of DESTRUCT!—the need to destroy technological civilization so as to cure the human race—was sincerely held, but many of his followers had their own interpretations and their own agendas.

The Guild did succeed, however, in releasing the abilities of some people to make use of what Blunt called the "Alternate Forces," and the Guild came into serious conflict with the established authorities who ran Earth, including above all the gigantic computer known as the Super-Complex.

During the course of the showdown that ultimately destroyed the influence of the Super-Complex, Blunt was removed from control of the Chantry Guild. In fact, the organization effectively shattered into a variety of groups, each seeking to go its own way.

Some of those groups were interested in little more than finding a means to make money. Other groups had other purposes and hung together to find what they desired. Largest of these rump Chantry Guilds was a group under the leadership of Jason Warren, who ultimately caused the formation of the Exotic "Splinter Culture."

The name "Chantry Guild" lay unused for the following two and a half centuries, until military forces of the Younger Worlds, led by the Others, invaded the two Exotic worlds, Mara and Kultis. Intending to totally destroy the Exotic culture and its people, the Others instituted severe controls over the Exotics, seeking ultimately to make it impossible for them to even live—much less to carry on their traditions and beliefs.

Quietly, nonviolently, some of the Exotics resisted, and among them was a group on Mara which, hidden in the mountains, sought a new path through a new form of meditation. They revived the name "Chantry Guild," and in the midst of destruction such as Walter Blunt had had in mind, began to create anew. They gave Hal Mayne the clue and direction he needed at a crisis point in his opposition to the Others.

JAMES CHILD-OF-GOD

A native of Harmony, James Child-of-God is one of those who still adheres to the dietary rules that were once decreed for most of the religious sects on the Friendly planets. Those rules, dating from a time when the Friendlies were so poor that everyone had to eat grass and weeds to stay alive, reflected a feeling that anything not absolutely required for survival must be a luxury that flew in the face of God's will.

To many off-worlders, such an attitude seems to be one of sheer, unreasoning fanaticism—and even some younger Friendlies refer to Child-of-God as an "Old Prophet." But while there is a certain condescension in the use of the term, there is also a grudging respect from people whose ways may be different but who recognize that Child-of-God sacrifices everything to follow the path to which he believes the Lord has called him.

James Child-of-God is an older man, gray-haired, with a lined, leathery face. Militant in his beliefs, he has spent much of his life in rebellion, in the midst of which his wife was killed by the planetary militia.

Child-of-God was one of those who recognized that the Friendly authorities were coming to be controlled by the Others. He is the sergeant and chief lieutenant of the command led by Rukh Tamani. He is opinionated and unyielding in his principles, and totally loyal to his Faith and to Rukh Tamani. His pale blue eyes can pierce like a diamond drill when his harsh, flat voice rips apart one's vanity, pride or self-delusion.

Although at times those same eyes can be as open and as innocent as those of a child, his commitment to his God is unwavering.

DOW deCASTRIES

Born in the mid-twenty-second century in southern China on Old Earth, Dow deCastries would in an earlier century have been called a Eurasian. He came from an extended family of mixed Portuguese and Chinese roots, a family of managers and business-men adept at supporting each other, as well as skilled at wielding political influence of the more hidden sorts.

Tall, slim, and elegant of manner, Dow was hand-some, with regular features and deep-set, dark eyes. His hair was dark and wavy, lightly touched with gray at the temples, and his voice was deep and mu-sical. He had great success with women, but men, too, were drawn to a certain air of power about him that mixed well with a thoughtful, almost abstracted, demeanor.

He rose rapidly in the turbulent politics of the Co-alition of Eastern Nations, one of the two main power blocs that competed for control of Earth and the Younger Worlds. After five years as secretary of Outworlds Affairs, he used Cletus Grahame's early successes in building the Dorsai into a military power to convince both the Coalition and its tradi-tional enemy, the Western Alliance, to give him the power to quash Grahame and the Dorsai.

It was deCastries' intention to parlay this delegation of power into personal control of both power blocs and, through them, of all the worlds. As always, he underestimated Grahame.

MICHAEL DE SANDOVAL

Third son of a family of High Island on the Dorsai, Michael de Sandoval grew up to be a big man, just a bit smaller than the Graeme twins. He was blond-haired and lean-faced, and displayed early a major talent for music.

Nonetheless, he seemed meant for success as a Dorsai soldier until—after graduating with honors from the Academy—he left the planet, refusing assignment to a military post, without explanation.

Some years later, he turned up on the planet Ceta as bandmaster of the Third Regiment of the Army of Nahar Colony. Other Dorsai working there learned that he had been fighting all his life to reconcile his Dorsai heritage with his deep feelings against hurting anything or anyone. On Gebel Nahar, that struggle came to a crisis.

THE DORSAI (culture)

More than any of the other Splinter Cultures, the Dorsai cannot be said to have arisen out of a particular group. For the Dorsai culture is based on the Dorsai *character*, which is the hyperdevelopment of an attitude and a psychological bias that was to be found in all groups and societies upon Earth.

Such characteristics could be found, for example,

in a man named Burton McLeod, who was a martial arts expert on Earth late in the twenty-first century. McLeod was a member of the Chantry Guild, and a friend and adviser to its founder, Walter Blunt. McLeod also became a friend of Paul Formain, the one-armed man who was to dislodge Blunt from his leadership role and change the direction of the Guild itself.

Expert with many weapons, McLeod was less a warrior than a protector. His mastery of the skills of violence was mated to a realization of his responsibility to use those skills in a moral fashion. And that responsibility was in turn rooted in McLeod's fidelity to a *tradition*—the tradition of the responsible warrior, and of duty, and of self-honor.

When the Chantry Guild was broken up, McLeod parted from Blunt and the others and went his own way. Where he went and what he did are not subject to available history, but it is clear that the attitude he exemplified has remained within the fiber of the human race and has been a part of the strength of the Dorsai culture.

The Dorsai culture did not create the Dorsai world; rather, the Dorsai world provided a fertile ground in which these particular characteristics could take root and grow into a culture.

It has been true throughout human history that hard times produce character. On the Dorsai, a group of people could survive only because they sent many of their men, in each generation, out to a heavy risk of being killed in other peoples' wars. The Dorsai is a poor planet, very much lacking in natural resources;

its people have nothing to sell except their abilities to fight. And they *had* to sell something, or they could not survive as a group, a planet, a culture. . . .

The people who came to the Dorsai came to find freedom, and they have never allowed that freedom to be abrogated. They continue to have only the most minimal government; this world has always been one on which any adult was free to go his own way, to make her own decisions. Every Dorsai is committed to a willingness to pay with his or her own life to buy freedom for the people; this decision was not reached only by the men who went out to fight—those who remained at home cherished the same image of freedom and were willing to die for it.

The Dorsai people, to continue in this fashion, had to pay a price. It was a high price, and it had to be paid continuously, generation after generation. On this world there could never be a hope that the war would end and the boys would come home.

One cannot be a Dorsai and not be aware of this. Every Dorsai knows that he owes what he has to the men and women who went before. A Dorsai cannot repay them except by passing the same gifts along to the next generation. So the Dorsai's is a strongly hereditary culture, for which tradition is a bond, a cement and a refuge.

In order to live such a life, the Dorsai must have the capacity to make the hard choices thrown at them. For a Dorsai, death is a better result than defeat—and this is not a decision they make as the occasion arises; rather, it is an attitude that is a part of their characters, their personalities. This leads to a calm certitude that is what others see as the Dorsai attitude.

Throughout human history there have been individuals—like Burton McLeod—who exemplified the creed of the moral warrior, who knew that with their power to fight came the imperative to use that power responsibly. And as the Dorsai people developed that ability to fight to a level never before seen, so, too, they developed the sense of responsibility to a level far above that known to the rest of mankind. On the Dorsai, there has developed a sense of Universal Responsibility; an unspoken commitment that is an integral part of the Dorsai character.

DORSAI WHISKY

An alcoholic beverage similar to a straight malt Scotch whiskey of Old Earth. Dorsai whisky (always spelled without the "e") is dark in color and very strong, with a smoky, pungent flavor and a fierce burn. It is the ceremonial drink of the Dorsai but is not popular on other worlds—which is just as well since the Dorsai cannot make much of it. And due to differences in the makeup of planets, the flavor cannot be duplicated on other worlds.

CORUNNA EL MAN

A Dorsai from High Island on the Dorsai, El Man is of Spanish heritage, and is tall and dark. He is skilled and a capable warrior, although his preference is to work with ships in space rather than on the surface of planets.

El Man lost his wife at the siege of Baunpore, when the city was overrun and a massacre resulted. The victorious troops killed her in front of him and then inflicted savage cuts on his face. He refused cosmetic surgery and goes through life with a hideously scarred face.

Some refer to him, in awe, as "He With Scars."

THE EXOTICS (culture)

The society that inhabits the planets Mara and Kultis, orbiting the star Procyon, is known to most of the rest of humanity as "the Exotics." Only the Friendlies refer to them by another name: "Deniers of God." And the Exotics themselves do not bother with such labels except when necessary for clear communication with off-worlders.

The seeds of Exotic society lay in human reactions to the rapid growth of technologically oriented civilization on Earth in the twentieth and twenty-first centuries. People trying to deal with feelings of vulnerability and insignificance sought refuge in a variety of what were sometimes called "alternate life-styles."

When Walter Blunt founded the Chantry Guild late in the twenty-first century, he provided an umbrella for a collection of groups and individuals with a wide variety of highly diverse philosophies and intentions—among them, for example, such ideas as yoga, the occult, Zen, holistic medicine, paranormal abilities, acupuncture, transcendental meditation; and such Eastern religions as Buddhism, Taoism, Hinduism and Modified Leninism, as well as Native American and Native Australian religions.

When the Chantry Guild fragmented, many of those people continued to associate with each other in a sort of "rump" Chantry Guild headed by the Necromancer Jason Warren. And early in the twenty-second century, they formalized their cooperation into an organization called the Association for the Investigation and Development of Exotic Sciences. It was this name, in shortened form, that ultimately led to the name given to their culture.

When the two planets nearest to Procyon were thrown open to immigration by the megacorporations that had been terraforming them, the Association funded the establishment of several colonies on the two worlds. Working together, those colonies prospered quickly; it was they who became prominent enough to *name* the two worlds.

Other groups had also colonized both worlds, and for much of the twenty-second century, inter-colony relations on each world largely reflected the battle for dominance that was being played out on Earth. Still dependent on Earth for financial and technological support, for markets and for immigrants, the colonies tended to accept protective relationships with one or the other of Earth's power blocs—and thus were drawn into brushfire wars and deeper dependency.

Recognizing this situation as the danger it was, the Exotics sought independence. It was they who fi-

nanced Cletus Grahame's revolution in warfare, and
they were rewarded when Grahame repaid their help,
both with money and by effectively destroying
Earth's military and political influence on the Younger Worlds.

The Exotics had realized early that independence
was necessary if they were to proceed on the course
they sought. They still represented among themselves
a variety of philosophies and intentions, but they had
in common a belief that humankind was yet in the
process of evolving into something better—and it
was their purpose to do what they could to monitor
that evolution and facilitate it.

To do that, they had to be and remain independent,
they realized. The Exotics determined to become
rich, which would be necessary to ensure that independence. They became proficient at a variety of
skills that the other worlds needed. They also used
their abilities to become one of the major powers in
interplanetary trade, dominating the trading routes so
as to keep others from doing so to the Exotics' dis-
advantage.

Independent, motivated by a purpose and highly
cooperative among themselves, the Exotic colonies
on Mara and Kultis prospered and grew quickly.
They soon overshadowed the non-Exotic colonies on
the two worlds, which either came around to an ap-
preciation of Exotic ideas and were absorbed or were
bought out and re-emigrated. (A few small groups
did remain on the planets, tolerated islands amid the
Exotic population.)

As has been mentioned, the Exotics contain among

themselves a wide variety of philosophies, but they are under no compulsion to conform to any standards or requirements. Each is free to search for, and work for, the future in the way he or she thinks best.

Off-worlders generally do not see such varieties, and so have a tendency to stereotype Exotics as a kind of genial Buddhist monk wandering about in loose robes and wreathed in gentle smiles. But in fact there are many sorts of Exotics—only their unity of purpose makes them a single people.

Cooperation is a given in the Exotic culture. When the community needs an Exotic's particular abilities, it finds them always available. And the community helps the individual, in turn, to improve himself, physically and mentally, so that he can be more effective in his work.

The Exotics believe that many paths may lead to the advancement of the human spirit, and they strenuously avoid putting pressures on their people to conform to any particular philosophy. Their culture has developed an innate capacity for seriously accepting an infinite number of possibilities, an attribute they call "multiconsideration."

Nonetheless, it may be said that, over time, certain characteristics have become common on their planets, providing a sort of "norm"—to which there are always exceptions.

Many Exotics are vegetarians. Most Exotic family structures are loose, the children being brought up to treat all adults almost equally as parent (or other relative) substitutes. And most Exotics approve of mixing ethnic strains rather than keeping them separate.

Among Exotics there is sometimes to be found a sort of generalized mysticism, perhaps to be expected of a society dedicated to the uplifting of the human race; more than other cultures, Exotics have seen indications of the powers possible to the human mind and spirit. But Exotics worship no god overtly and follow no religion; in fact, to the Friendlies, some Exotics have seemed aggressively atheistic in philosophy, particularly in the belief that religious dogmatism retards human evolution—which is why the Friendlies call them the "Deniers of God."

Most of the other human worlds tend to see the Exotics as pacifists, dedicated to nonviolence for moral reasons. This picture is erroneous. The Exotics in fact have little moral objection to fighting, and when they need to fight, they hire the very best mercenaries to handle the chore for them—hence the long and mutually profitable relationship they have maintained with the Dorsai.

Exotics *themselves* avoid fighting, because involvement in fights tends to lead to a variety of emotional tensions and releases that interfere with clear thinking. No Exotic is under any compulsion not to touch weapons, but almost all of them believe that the use of force damages the individual's ability to do his or her work.

Some Exotics subscribe to a principle of noninterference, feeling that it is violence to even urge a point of view upon another person. But if Exotics are averse to doing violence to others, they also believe that no one should be permitted to do violence to *them*.

The Exotics, wishing to help improve the human race, believe that one of the paths to betterment is the improvement of the individual human being. One of the reasons they had for seeking wealth was simply that in being rich, they could avoid having to struggle for a living—thus freeing themselves and their minds to search for the improvement of the race.

For similar reasons, they seek to make the individual human as healthy as possible, in all ways. They are, to the rest of the worlds, virtual wizards in the healing arts—physically, psychologically and emotionally. Their life-styles—even their architecture—reflect such considerations. Exotics generally do not keep pets, for instance, eschewing the emotional involvements inherent in the practice; but they will sometimes use colorful fish in pools to enhance the feelings of harmony and peace that they like to design into their living spaces.

The Exotics have also worked extensively in genetic research and feel no compunction about trying to improve the race by using that tool, too, upon themselves. Having made it a principle to avoid the emotional side effects inherent to romantic entanglements and in familial relationships, many of the Exotics have procreated, as it were, to order. As a result, most Exotics are healthy, regular of feature and intelligent; they seem distinctive to much of the rest of the race, having blended a variety of ethnic strains, although they have by no means achieved a uniformity of appearance.

The principles of cooperation that they espouse, and their avoidance of the use of force, have meant that the two Exotic planets have only the most minimal of government or governing bodies. For the most part, Exotics allow decisions that affect all of them to be handled by those in whose fields they lie. Naturally, others can object at any time; if they do, the effort made to accommodate all sides is enormous, until consensus can be achieved. It is this attitude that has led some to describe one Exotic cultural trait as the "relentless Exotic courtesy"—a combination of implications that are both true of their society.

More than any society in history, the Exotic culture can be characterized as being one of philosophers. But the other human societies have never fully recognized what this means.

It means that while no Exotic sheds blood, they all dream of a future—a future that *must* mean the obliteration of the present. In this regard, the Exotics remain true, in their fashion, to the message of Walter Blunt, whose program was DESTRUCT! In their philosophies, the Exotics still desire destruction, to make room for something different to appear on the human stage.

For all their individual courtesy and gentleness, the Exotics are ruthless.

They are ruthless simply because they are philosophers. Philosophers are ruthless, even toward themselves, because philosophers are ruled by theory alone, and theories allow no weaknesses. As has been said, the Exotics are courteous—and even their courtesy is relentless.

There have been those among the rest of the human race who have wondered if the Exotics are still fully human. . . .

THE FINAL ENCYCLOPEDIA

Conceived of early in the twenty-third century by the Earthman Mark Torre, the Encyclopedia was intended to be more than just a storehouse of all human knowledge. Torre convinced Earth to begin the project, in hopes that the discoveries it made could benefit the planet in future interstellar transactions.

However, the peoples of the culture on the two Exotic worlds came quickly to appreciate the possible value of the Encyclopedia also. The Exotics did not wholly agree with Mark Torre's theory that humanity had already evolved itself; they believed that humanity *would* evolve—and they felt that the Encyclopedia might play a role in such development. For decades, the Exotics provided the major funding in support of the project, although they took no ownership role.

Construction of the Final Encyclopedia began in the year 2228, on the ground in the Exotic Enclave near St. Louis, in North America upon Earth. It was begun on the ground as a spread-out complex of structures planned, when moved into space, to fold up into a spherical shape.

The Encyclopedia was designed to hold all available facts and then to link those facts, via pulses of energy, in an effort to discover relationships between them—relationships previously unknown. Torre's hope was that this would enable mankind to learn something about itself, something it had not been able to see on its own ... Torre referred to a blind area, analogous to a man trying to see the back of his own head. No one was able to guess in advance what such knowledge might be.

Although the Final Encyclopedia was technically controlled by a Board of Governors, Torre—and Tam Olyn after him—was able to control the board and direct the building in accordance with his vision. During Tam's term as Director of the Encyclopedia, the project was raised into a near-Earth orbit, folded into a spheroid and surrounded with a phase shield for protection—which appears to the eye as a wall of gray fog.

Construction continued within that shield while the Encyclopedia used its own drive engines to hold itself steadily above one spot on Earth, a case of dynamic geosynchronicity.

It was from the base of the Final Encyclopedia that the effort to protect Earth from the forces of the Others was directed, as Hal Mayne succeeded Tam Olyn as Director.

FORALIE

A District of Caerlon Island on the Dorsai, it is also the town in that District. Both took their name from Foralie homestead, which lies over a ridge from the town.

Foralie homestead was established by an immigrant to the Dorsai, an exiled British-Afghanistani general named Eachan Khan. His wife, Shauna Gray, was Scottish by birth, and named the homestead for the place in Scotland where she grew up. The name was later extended to the nearby small town, and then to the District.

Foralie homestead was sited in a pleasant, green, sheltered place among the trees, near Lake Athan. When Cletus Grahame came to the Dorsai, he lived at Foralie for a while, before building his own home, Grahamehouse, less than half a mile up the slope. As was typical of Grahame's military thinking, his house was placed on a bare piece of earth on a high perch, exposed to the winds and snow.

After Cletus married Eachan Khan's daughter Melissa, the old general came to live with them at Grahamehouse. One night the original house burned down; it was never rebuilt, and since then, Grahamehouse (later to be spelled "Graemehouse") has been Foralie, too.

PAUL FORMAIN

A young American of the late twenty-first century, Formain was involved in a boat accident at the age of eighteen. He came away from the incident with dreams that he had actually died and been brought back to life by a mysterious, caped figure wearing a tall hat. His psychotherapists felt that he was trying to explain away to himself the failure of a suicide attempt.

Formain went on to earn a mining degree and then took a job directing automatic mining machinery in the Canadian Rockies. Large-boned, tall and athletic, with warm gray eyes, a friendly mouth and straight, light brown hair, he seemed a normal young man. But on his first day on the job, he had an accident that cost him his left arm.

Attempts to give him a new arm by means of a transplant failed, but in the meantime, his right arm, in compensation, became unusually large and strong. Eight months after his accident, he went to Chicago to make contact with the Chantry Guild, an organization whose members claimed immense powers, including the power to replace Paul's arm.

Paul Formain found himself embroiled with a mysterious group of people as a chess piece in their war with the Super-Complex, the great computer that ruled the world. But while working his way to an understanding of this situation, he found that he himself had great powers.

At the showdown, Formain turned the tables on Walter Blunt, the Guildmaster, who thought he had created and was using Paul. But the end revealed that Paul was actually working for another power, out of mankind's future.

THE FRIENDLIES

"Friendlies" is the name given, in sardonic fashion, to the culture that resides on the pair of worlds, Harmony and Association, orbiting the star Epsilon Eridani. The people of these two worlds have an in-

terstellar reputation as humorless, ultra-religious fanatics, and they have scant friends or admirers across
human-inhabited space. Few recall that there was a
time, long ago, when "Friends" was a kindly reference to certain gentle, devout religious groups.

The Friendly culture had its origin on Earth, where
late in the twenty-first century, large numbers of people found refuge from the pressures and terrors of
technological civilization in "marching societies."
These groups would periodically meet to join in a
group trek, on foot—treks often characterized by
mass outbursts of religious hysteria.

Early in the twenty-second century, many of these
groups determined to leave an Earth that was largely
unsympathetic to their fervor, and the opportunity to
do so came when two worlds orbiting E. Eridani
were declared open for colonization by the conglom-
erate that had been terraforming them.

These two worlds were known to be badly lacking
in natural resources, and so colonization licenses
were not in great demand. This seemed an attractive
feature to many Earthbound religious groups, who
felt that the lack of natural wealth would help to
keep their people from the temptations of the flesh. It
would also discourage nonreligious people from
coming to these worlds.

Combining their resources, a coalition of disparate
religious groups bought exclusive colonization rights
to the two planets and—perhaps in the hope of min-
imizing future inter-sect conflict—named the two
planets Harmony and Association.

The price of interstellar travel being high, many of

the members of these groups never got off Earth, but satisfied themselves with the hope that they had given their all to further the growth of a new, God-fearing culture. Eventually, these Earthbound lost all touch with those they had sent out.

Those who went to the new worlds did so packed tightly into ships and with the barest minimum of equipment. Generally farmers for reasons having to do with religious fundamentalism as well as with lack of education, they found themselves struggling to hack out farms and build churches from thin, stony soil.

Poor when they arrived, they generally remained poor, and many died. Those who survived struggled, for generations, for barest subsistence, and it took more than a century for the planets to begin to be able to afford a few rudiments of modern technology.

The Friendlies came to their planets in small groups. Each group represented an individual religious sect; for the most part, a wide variety of Christian groups, although there were some groups that combined Christian traditions with Muslim, Jewish or Buddhist ideas.

Between the worlds there is a saying that every Friendly is a sect unto himself. This proved almost literally true soon after colonization began, and the history of the two planets is one of the continual splintering, growth and resplintering of the religious groups on their surfaces.

These splinterings were frequently violent in nature and at times led to open warfare. The planetary governments, subject to their own ideological strains and often lacking resources, had difficulty dealing with inter-sect guerrilla warfare and sometimes had to expend vital, hard-to-accumulate wealth to hire professional soldiery from off-planet.

Each Friendly world is governed in ostensibly democratic fashion by an elected legislative assembly and a chief executive—usually chosen on the basis of the voting of religious blocs. But for purposes of presenting a united front to the unbelievers on other worlds, the planetary chief executive who has received the most votes in the most recent planetary elections represents both planets in interstellar affairs. He is called the Eldest and is First of the United Council of Churches, which rules from Government Center on Harmony. Governing two such unstable planets calls for the strongest of personalities and wills. The best-known of such leaders was Eldest Bright, who bent the two planets to his will over the course of three decades in the late twenty-third century.

Lacking natural resources, Friendly leaders found that the things that grew best on their two planets were people. If they could subsist at all, Friendlies tended to raise large families, and the lack of medical technologies was balanced by the scarcity of infectious disease and the healthy effects of an industrious, spartan life-style. Certain mineral and vitamin supplements were necessary due to lacks in the planetary ecologies; once provided, hard work and simple foods kept people healthy.

The Friendly worlds quickly found that they had nothing to offer worth the cost of export in interstellar trade; all they had were people, and those tended to be undereducated—valueless to others except as mercenary soldiers.

Starved for interstellar currency, the Friendlies took to drafting their young men for wars on other planets. These soldiers, young and poorly trained, were at best simple cannon fodder. They had the ability to shoot, though, and could be counted on to obey orders. They took up a gun as they would a plow or a shovel—as a tool to be used for their people and their church.

Untrained, they tended to die quickly and to be replaced by a new crop of draftees. Those few who managed to survive long enough might eventually become good soldiers. (Those with experience in inter-sect fighting soon became better soldiers than their drafted brethren.)

For the first two centuries, interstellar opinion tended to regard Friendlies as sour, humorless, religious fanatics, given to hair shirts, prayer and arguments. But over time, some people began to recognize that while many Friendlies were, indeed, fanatics—people who use their concepts of God and worship to serve, even if unconsciously, their own desires—others were what came to be called True Faith-holders, i.e., people who followed the path their faith saw as right, regardless of its cost.

It is this pure, strong faith that is the bloom of the Friendly culture, the end product of three centuries of lives on two worlds—and the gift of the Friendlies to the future of the human race.

DONAL GRAEME

Great-great-grandson of Cletus Grahame and younger son of Eachan Khan Graeme, Donal Graeme was born on the Dorsai in the middle of the twenty-third century. He grew up to be a sizable man, but small for a Dorsai, and particularly for his unusual family.

He was slim, but displayed the strength, reflexes and smoothness of movement endowed by Dorsai genes and training. His face was sharp and angular, straight-nosed; his hair was black, straight, and a little coarse. The most unusual thing to be seen about him was his eyes, which seemed to have no particular color, but looked gray or green or blue. . . .

The pivotal event of Donal Graeme's life came before he was a teenager with the death and funeral of his beloved Uncle James. James had died in battle after a betrayal; it was an unnecessary death, which plunged the boy into a cold rage. He dedicated himself to changing the system that caused such deaths.

In the following years, he graduated from the Dorsai Academy and purposely set out to make a name for himself among the worlds so that he could gain the power to alter the system. He had the advantage of possessing unusual mental talents of such scope that it might well be said that he was a mutant, a significant step forward in the evolution of humankind.

At an extraordinarily young age, Graeme became Protector of the Worlds—and began to understand that while he could enforce peace and the rule of law on the planets, he had not changed a single mind or a single attitude in the base structure of the human animal.

He saw that his plan to mend the race had not succeeded, because he himself was flawed by the isolation from other humans that had been with him all his life.

He began again.

IAN GRAEME

Great-grandson of Cletus Grahame, Ian was the twin of Kensie, and younger brother of Eachan Khan Graeme. Like Kensie, Ian was tall, lean, dark of hair and deeply tanned, with a big-boned face. Both Kensie and Ian had the Dorsai characteristic of displaying an utter stillness when at rest—and a startling swiftness when in motion.

Ian is a superbly trained fighter, muscular and a deadly weapon all by himself. But he is above all a master strategist, as well as a renowned trainer of troops.

All who have met Ian and his twin have commented upon the fact that while Kensie seemed to project feelings of warmth and joy, Ian seemed to radiate cold and darkness. Tam Olyn, coming upon Ian unexpectedly, described him as "Kensie with murder on his mind."

It was not that Ian actually *was* a grim, heartless man; it was only that he seemed somehow to be psychologically bound to his twin in an unusual fashion. It was as if Ian and Kensie formed one person, and

Ian by himself could only be half that person—and all the warmth and light was in the other half.

Non-Dorsai often misread Ian's personality, seeing him as remote, uncaring and bleak of soul. Dorsai knew better, and read and respected Ian, for all his fierce and lonely demeanor, as a true Dorsai warrior and the best man of war of them all.

KENSIE GRAEME

Twin brother of Ian and younger brother of Eachan Khan Graeme (the father of Donal Graeme), Kensie was in appearance identical to Ian; lean, tall even for Dorsai, with slightly curly, coarse black hair and a big-boned face containing brilliant gray-green eyes.

Slim and strong, well-muscled for all his leanness, and a superbly trained fighter with lightning reflexes, Kensie was also a master tactician. His abilities were recognized by all, including the Exotics, who, able to hire only the best, repeatedly called him in to solve problems for them. He often worked in tandem with his twin, a great strategist.

Non-Dorsai often find a certain feeling of security in the presence of a Dorsai; it was said of the twins that even other Dorsai had this feeling when around them. Both were the finest exemplars of what has come to be called the Dorsai character.

In very un-Dorsai fashion—and even unlike his twin—Kensie Graeme had a special, unique personality that was recognized by all. He seemed to radiate a powerful feeling of sunny warmth, which flowed like sunshine out onto those around him. Others felt happy to be near him, using terms such as "a golden god of the sunshine," for all that he was black of hair and darkly tanned.

Even though he was unlucky in love, he never lost that special radiance. He died in an ambush on Ste. Marie.

CLETUS GRAHAME

Born in the middle of the twenty-second century in the United States, on Old Earth, Grahame came from an old military family which remembered that its name had been Americanized. Later, he would return it to its ancient spelling.

Related to generals, Cletus nevertheless wanted to be a painter. But when his number came up in the draft, he decided after all to go to the Military Academy, as his family had always wanted him to do.

After graduating with honors, he was commissioned into the military forces of the Western Alliance and shortly found himself in battle in a brushfire war with Coalition forces on the island of Java. There he won the Medal of Honor, but also took a wound that left him with a partially prosthetic left knee, which continued to trouble him at times.

Thereafter he was held out of action and became an instructor at the Military Academy. While there, he began writing the first books of a projected multivolume work on tactics and strategies.

Tall and lean, he found that his open features and cheerful, harmless look kept people from taking his writings seriously. He decided that he needed to enhance his reputation, so he requested a transfer to the Alliance's Expeditionary Forces defending Bakhalla Colony on Kultis. There, in a series of brilliant small actions, and in the face of serious opposition by his superiors, he destroyed the enemy as an effective military force. He also made himself the major foe of a high-ranking Coalition political boss, Dow deCastries.

Resigning his commission and his Alliance citizenship, Grahame emigrated to the Dorsai while recovering from a miraculous cure of his damaged knee, performed by his own mental powers. There he set up a complete retraining program for the Dorsai professional soldiers, thereby multiplying their effectiveness.

He led the Dorsai troops in a series of military campaigns that not only gave the soldiers an increased value on the professional military market, but made him a figure so notorious that deCastries could use him as a threat to Old Earth. The forces of both Alliance and Coalition united in a campaign to destroy the Dorsai reputation and then conquer their planet.

Cletus Grahame, however, had foreseen all of this, and when he defeated deCastries' troops, it spelled the end of Earth's hopes of dominating the Younger Worlds. Those worlds would now be set free to work out their own destinies without Earth's influence.

Grahame completed the writing of his twenty-volume work; it, together with his training program, made the incredible effectiveness of the Dorsai soldiers possible. Officially entitled "Theory of Tactics and Strategical Considerations," it is often refered to as "The Tactics of Mistake."

Cletus Grahame may justifiably be called the Napoleon of his era; few understand, however, that the most important part of his genius lay in his ability to impart his own military skills to others.

THE GREY CAPTAINS

The Dorsai has no planetary government in generally accepted meanings of the term. But the Dorsai people, knowing and working closely with each other, sometimes come to respect particular individuals as natural leaders.

The concept of a "Grey Captain" has developed over the course of the centuries. During the time of Cletus Grahame, for instance, there were individuals who were accepted leaders—but the term "Grey Captain" was not yet in existence.

There is no organization of "Grey Captains," and there is no process of election or selection to such a post. It is simply that many people recognize a particular woman or man as a leader, as someone whom others trust, and trust to make decisions.

Because the primary business of the Dorsai is the work of the mercenary soldiers, the Dorsai is the only planet whose people often make contracts directly with off-planet governments and organizations. An accepted, trusted leader with the power to get such a contract will in turn subcontract with other Dorsai to help fulfill the contract—and so the Grey

Captains are usually (not always) such contractors, men and women who have been leaders of fighting forces.

The Grey Captains have no power to make decisions for the Dorsai. But if many of these leaders recommend a particular course of action, much of the planet will go along.

INTERSTELLAR CURRENCY

During an era when the cost of interstellar transportation is very high, the most valuable—and easily portable—commodity is knowledge, especially knowledge in the form of the expertise that resides in the minds of highly trained people. Since most planets cannot afford to train all the specialists they need, they have tended to specialize in particular fields. Thus, the Dorsai produce the best professional soldiers, and the Friendlies cannon fodder; Newton produces the best physicists, and the Exotics the best physicians—and so on.

In practice, a value is placed on experts, and worlds that export one sort of expert can build up a credit balance, which they can then use to purchase the services of others' specialists as they need them. (In addition, most worlds maintain a system of planetary currency, but it is usually not convertible to other currencies.)

Because minds with specialized training had become so important to most worlds' prosperity—perhaps even to their survival—some worlds responded by virtually enslaving their peoples. These worlds, during the twenty-third century, were called "tight," because the individual citizen signed to a personal services contract was at the orders of his authorities, with no say as to when his contract was sold or traded, and he with it. He or she was tightly bound.

In contrast, on the "loose" contract worlds, a contracted citizen retained a certain ownership of her own contract, and she could not be sold or traded without her consent—except in emergency conditions.

Thus, between worlds, people were either non-free or partly free.

For the most part, those worlds carrying out a "tight contract" policy were the Friendlies, Newton, Cassida, Venus, Coby and Ceta. The "loose contract" side included the Exotics, the Dorsai, Earth, Mars, New Earth, Freiland and Ste. Marie.

The harsh system was ameliorated somewhat after Donal Graeme crushed the attempt by William of Ceta to corner the labor market and take control of the worlds.

KANTELE

Born late in the twenty-first century, Kantele Maki became a popular vocalist while still quite young and was widely known simply by her first name. "Kantele" was a name from the Finnish national epic, the Kaleva—the name of the sacred harp, a harp for the hands of gods or heroes.

Kantele was an American of Finnish descent, tall

and slim, pale in complexion, with fine-cut features and blue eyes. In earlier centuries, many of the peoples of northern Europe felt that the Finns were a people of witches.

Kantele was a member of the Chantry Guild, and she was in love with the organization's founder, Walter Blunt.

EZEKIEL MACLEAN

The younger brother of Henry MacLean, Ezekiel is very unlike his brother. Born a Friendly on Association, Ezekiel abandoned the Friendly culture and the whole question of Faith.

Ezekiel is a warm, gentle, easygoing man, the exact opposite of how the Friendlies are regarded by most people. Out among the stars, he gets along well with others, including an expatriate Exotic woman who was making her way from man to man. Ezekiel was her lover for a while, and even when shut out of her bedroom, he hung around, half-friend and half-servant.

When the Exotic wanted to be rid of her older son, Dahno Ahrens, Ezekiel took responsibility for the young man and convinced his brother Henry to take in the boy. Later, Ezekiel performed the same service for the younger boy, Bleys Ahrens.

Until Bleys was in his turn shipped off to Association, Ezekiel was the boy's only approach to friendship.

■ *Gordon R. Dickson*

HENRY MACLEAN

Henry MacLean (pronounced "MaClain" in the Scottish fashion) is a Friendly, a devout practitioner of his religion, who lives on a small, poor farm on the planet Association. He is tall and very thin, with a narrow face and dark eyes. His voice is a light baritone in pitch, but his manner makes it seem rusty and harsh.

Henry is now somewhere in middle age, although it is hard to determine his years by his appearance, his hair being rather drab in color. In his youth he was once drafted to fight off-planet, and later he became a Soldier of God, one of those Friendlies who frequently get themselves involved in the conflicts—ranging from skirmishes to minor wars—between sects that are common on the Friendly planets.

One day he found that he did not trust himself to fight with a pure heart; afraid he might be coming to *like* fighting, he quit and returned to farming. He now will not touch a weapon if he can help it.

Widowed, Henry raises goats with his two young sons. The farm is poor, but Henry was willing to take in first Dahno, then Bleys, at the request of Ezekiel, Henry's apostate brother.

Henry MacLean often has a harsh manner and an impatient air, but there are those who know that his gruffness can hide an inner kindness. But the most important thing in his life is his Faith; he impresses some as a religious fanatic, but he is truly devout.

ANEA MARLIVANA

A native of Kultis, she was the product of generations of Exotic genetic selection and psychological techniques. The Exotics called her the Select of Kultis, meaning that she was considered their best result in her generation. To them, this meant that she had within herself the capacity to be healthy and intelligent and to live life more fully than most.

They gave her the capacity; what she did with it was then up to her.

The result was a tall, slim young lady who gave clear promise that she would one day be beautiful. But, contracted to serve as part of the entourage of William of Ceta, her life became troubled and confused as she became a target of his machinations.

When William was quashed, Anea married Donal Graeme. They had no children at the time Donal vanished while in a phase shift.

After a while, Anea returned to the Exotic worlds, where eventually she was married to someone else, for the preservation of her genes.

HAL MAYNE

Near the middle of the twenty-fourth century, a courier spacecraft was found floating, undriven, in space near Earth, with no one on board except a two-year-old boy. Along with him were instructions that the craft was to be sold and its proceeds used to raise the boy under the care of three tutors, those to be a Dorsai, a Friendly and an Exotic.

Fourteen years later, the boy's elderly tutors were killed by gunmen in the employ of the Others. The boy, Hal Mayne, escaped from Earth to the Final Encyclopedia. There he came to the attention of Tam Olyn, aged Director of the Encyclopedia, who asked him to stay to learn how to run the installation. The boy refused and went out into the Younger Worlds, to continue running from the Others, while growing up.

He became tall and strong, with wide shoulders and black hair. His eyes are green, set beneath a wide forehead. His face is strong-boned, his nose straight above a level mouth.

The mystery of Hal's origin is deeper than anyone knew; he himself was not to realize the truth about himself until he had grown, learned about life and his fellow humans, and gone through his own particular rite of passage. Battling through to the truth about himself was an agonizing, shocking process; but he became the man who could design and lead the defense of Earth.

AMANDA MORGAN (I)

A native of Wales, born on Old Earth near the end of the twenty-first century, Amanda Morgan grew to be an intelligent, imaginative, tall young woman, her beautiful, regular features framed by white-blond hair.

Amanda married a young man of a rich, powerful family. But her husband, Lloyd Jones, died, and when their baby, Jimmy, was six months old, Jones's family had the child legally taken from her. For four years she fought the situation, finally winning visiting rights. Then she took the baby and fled from Earth.

She went to Newton, then in its earliest years of settlement, and remarried. Here she found that Jimmy had been psychologically damaged and was given to sudden, near-psychotic outbursts of fury and rash decisions. Amanda was never to know whether these were the result of her in-laws' handling or of something in their genes. But she determined to protect her son from himself, all his life.

When Jimmy was half-grown, Amanda's second husband died and she emigrated to the Dorsai. The world was just opening up, and she was one of the first permanent settlers. She built her house, Fal Morgan, which became the family homestead.

During what became known as the Outlaw Years, Amanda was a local leader in the battle to bring under control the groups of renegade mercenary soldiers who, camping in the mountains, preyed on farms and small towns during the periods when the men there were away. Never a mercenary soldier herself, she nonetheless fought when it was necessary, refusing to let anyone at all impinge upon her rights.

On the Dorsai, she married for a third time. She had more children, but the focus of her life was firmly fixed on her family as a group, and on the people around her. She kept Jimmy with her for all his life, guarding and controlling him until his death. His children became the line of the ap Morgans; large men who were professional soldiers before the

Graemes ever made a name for themselves on the Dorsai.

Amanda Morgan was old when Eachan Khan and his family immigrated to the Dorsai and established Foralie homestead; older still—in her nineties—when Cletus Grahame came. Nonetheless, she was the one the people called on for leadership when Grahame had to be gone while the Earth forces of Dow deCastries invaded the Dorsai.

In later years, people began to recognize that there was a particular Dorsai *character*—and that Amanda Morgan was Dorsai before there was a Dorsai world. She did not always like it that she was so often called upon to decide, to discipline, to carry out distasteful jobs; but she always recognized the jobs that *had* to be done. She would not let any of them best her.

AMANDA MORGAN (II)

Born nearly fifty years after the death of her great-great-great grandmother, the first Amanda, the second Amanda was actually christened Elaine by her parents, Alban and Millicent ap Morgan. But before she was six years old, people began to call her Amanda because she reminded them so much of the stories of the legendary founder of the family. Later, it would be said that she named herself.

The ap Morgans were next neighbors of the Graemes, in Foralie District on the Dorsai; and Elaine/Amanda grew up with the Graeme twins, Kensie and Ian. Both boys fell in love with her, and she thought she was in love with Kensie when the twins left the planet to follow the Dorsai trade. Later, she came to feel otherwise.

Amanda became in time her planet's primary authority on mercenary contracts, but unable to reconcile her personal needs with her perceived duty to her planet and her people, she decided to marry no one.

She lived to the age of a hundred and six. She would become the great grandaunt of the third Amanda, whose rearing she would oversee.

The second Amanda was nearly identical to the first in appearance, and like her, lived a long life but never showed her age.

AMANDA MORGAN (III)

Eldest daughter of Thomas Morgan and Delia White, and great granddaughter of Charley Morgan, who was with Kensie Graeme when he died, the third Amanda was given her name by her great grandaunt, the second Amanda. In fact, the strong-willed second Amanda practically co-opted the little girl and directed much of her upbringing.

The third Amanda bears an amazing physical resemblance to the first two; she is tall and athletic, slim and erect, with shoulder-length white-blond hair framing turquoise eyes that seem to change color with her moods—or perhaps it is the light.

She is the Dorsai's leading expert on contracts, but has been fully trained in Dorsai military skills. She has also inherited the ap Morgan gift for *seeing*, at times, things that others cannot perceive.

TAM OLYN

An Earthman of Irish ancestry, Tam Olyn, with his younger sister Eileen, was raised by their uncle, Mathias Olyn, after being orphaned by an air-car crash. Mathias was a disciple of Walter Blunt, the founder of the Chantry Guild in the twenty-first century, but by the mid-twenty-third century, Mathias had interpreted Blunt's message as one of futility and despair.

Eager to escape Mathias's oppressive nihilism, Tam became a star student at the best postgraduate journalism school in human space and, upon graduation, joined the Interstellar News Services as a trainee. Tam's intention was to achieve for himself the freedom and power that newsmen enjoyed during an era when most people were subject to governmental and industrial controls.

At that point, during a visit to the Final Encyclopedia, Tam underwent a psychic experience that brought him to the attention of the man who ran the Encyclopedia, Mark Torre. Torre, along with his assistant, Lisa Kant, asked Tam to help with the Encyclopedia project. But Tam, suffused with the newfound realization of his own personal power, refused and set out on a course to manipulate the world and the people about him.

Tam's efforts led to a series of tragedies and deaths, until he came to realize that he had been merely reprising his own inner urge to destruction. He turned his life around and used his abilities to further the Encyclopedia project, even into his extreme old age—he was well over a hundred and twenty years old when he finally found a successor to take over his beloved Encyclopedia.

His life was lived in atonement for the evils he had done; at the end of it, he found the self-forgiveness he needed.

ONTOGENETICS

Ontogenetics is a science—or possibly an art—that has been developed by the Exotics as part of their quest to study and advance human evolution.

Exotic theorists began their search by trying to pile up as much knowledge as possible (a motive, too, for their support of the Final Encyclopedia project), looking for clues that might show a pattern leading to the evolved form of humanity.

In time, Exotic calculative techniques began to reveal an ongoing pattern of events in history, in which all living human beings are caught up. In mass, the strivings and desires of people determine the growth of the pattern into the future—although, as individuals, most people are more acted upon by the pattern than act effectively upon it.

In theory, such calculations must include every human being upon all the worlds, as well as all of the forces that impinge upon them; these calculations are further modified by the effects that such human institutions as societies themselves have upon the pattern and the people.

In practice, the Exotics have found that certain individuals may be more influential upon the patterns than others; this influence may or may not coincide with these individuals' effect upon the history of their time. The Exotic science is far from exact, but it attempts to identify such people and study them closely.

At the same time, Exotic ontogeneticists try very hard to keep a low profile about their studies. They fear that publicity, or the *tagging* of certain individuals as influential, may prejudice the actions of such people, and of those around them.

The science is still quite tenuous—it miscalculated Donal Graeme, for one—and its practitioners are constantly embroiled in controversy.

THE OTHERS

The origin of the group that came to be called "the Others" is shrouded in mystery, in part because of a clever disinformation campaign conducted by later leaders of the group, and in part because it was a highly informal and unstructured body of people. Sometimes they called themselves the "Other People," or the "New People."

It appears that the group had its origin in a sort of social club that functioned as a support group for people whose parents came from one or more than one of the Splinter Cultures. Such people, raised in two or more of the Splinter Cultures at once, sometimes had difficulty fitting into more conventional society.

The idea of such a group may have begun on Ceta early in the twenty-fourth century; similar groups sprang up on other planets, but they were not organized so as to maintain any contact with each other.

In the middle of the century, such a group in Ecumeny, capital city of the planet Association, was approached by a young man named Dahno Ahrens. Armed with a great intelligence as well as an astounding ability to charm his listeners, Dahno took over the local group. He motivated the unhappy young half-breeds he found with a vision of personal wealth and power, to be achieved by letting him direct their education and efforts.

Himself extremely successful as a political lobbyist and adviser, Dahno rose rapidly to become a hidden power in the planet's affairs. And as he continued recruiting more young Others, he was able to teach them to set up similar positions on other planets.

Until this time, the Others—and Dahno himself—were intent on little more than setting themselves up in lucrative positions. At this point, Dahno's younger brother, Bleys Ahrens, stepped in.

Bleys was himself already possessed by a vision of a larger future and had determined to use his brother's organization to achieve it. Intelligent, striking in appearance and a fine psychologist, he had worked hard to make himself persuasive and charismatic, even though he lacked his half-brother's natural talent in that regard.

Bleys went to the Others' suborganizations on a number of the Younger Worlds and converted them to his own ends by selling the local Others a vision of their own ability to rule all the Younger Worlds. He excited them and led them into a drive to vastly expand the Others' organization and their control of the worlds.

The Others are relatively few in number as compared to the billions of people on the planets. But their influence is immensely magnified by the fact that each of them controls a network of ordinary people who are themselves influential in the affairs of their various planets.

At the base of the extraordinary influence of the Others lies their power of persuasion. The supreme practitioner of this art is Dahno Ahrens, but many Others have some of this ability if properly trained to use it.

It appears that this power of persuasion may be a result to some extent of the Friendly culture itself, which has always put a premium on proselytization and preaching. With proper training upon a basis of this culturally endowed power, an Other may be able to persuade people to follow his or her lead. But these powers do not seem to work upon people of the Dorsai or Exotic cultures.

Led by Bleys' intelligence and will, supported by Dahno's ability to charm and persuade, the Others— themselves already persuaded—turn in their turn to convincing people to go along with them. They rule most of the Younger Worlds simply because they rule those world's rulers.

PADMA

A native of Mara, Padma is considered by many to be the perfect exemplar of the Exotic culture. Habitually dressed in robes of various shades of blue, with hair white from a young age, he always impresses people with a sense of calm and peace. He has an ageless look that has led others to regard him as a modern image of a Buddha.

Unquestionably brilliant, Padma is in fact not a "typical" Exotic; it might be more accurate to call him the outstanding blossom of the Exotic culture: a strong, intelligent individual, always moving purposefully toward the goal that is the reason-for-being of his people.

PHASE SHIFT

The beginnings of phase-shift technology were developed by Operation Springboard on Earth late in the twenty-first century. The first experiments led to the establishment of a station on Mercury, closest planet to Earth's sun, which worked with the Super-Complex computer on Earth.

The basis of the work started with the Heisenberg Uncertainty Principle, a long-known phenomenon. According to the principle, it is impossible to determine at the same moment both the position and the velocity of a particle in the universe with full accuracy. In fact, the more accurately you may know one of those factors, the more uncertain will be your knowledge of the other.

This may be stated another way: there is a reciprocal relationship between time and position, such that if time becomes nonexistent ("inoperative" might be a better word), the choice of position becomes infinite. It is this "no-time" or "a-time" state that is the basis of the phase shift, because velocity is a function of time.

From this principle was developed the phase drive, or phase-shift drive, used by spaceships to travel across interstellar space. It is more correct to say, however, that spaceships do not actually *move* by means of the phase shift. Rather, they simply abandon one position and appear in another, a phenomenon suggestive of fantasies of teleportation.

What actually happens is that a ship that activates its phase-shift field can, in an "instant" of no-time, absolutely fix its velocity. During that "instant," then, its position reciprocally becomes universal. And when the "instant" of no-time ends, the ship can, by proper manipulation of the fields, return from *universal* position to a *particular* position in a new location.

Thus, a ship under phase-shift drive does not actually *move*; rather, it changes the mathematical description of its position in the universe. At the actual moment of shift, a ship is, theoretically, spread out evenly throughout the universe—and then immediately reassembled at some other designated spot than that which it occupied an instant before.

In other words, the ship has "restated" its position in the universe. A ship abandons one defined position, becomes undefined, and then redefines itself at a new position.

Unfortunately, it appears that the greater the space-time distance disregarded by a particular restatement, the more uncertain will become the point at which the ship returns to ordinary space-time existence. Safe travel requires intense, difficult calculations, and recalculation of a ship's position every time a shift is made.

Justifiably, there is great fear that a ship will shift to a position that it cannot recognize—in other words, will not know where it has arrived. If that should happen, a ship will be irretrievably lost in the infinities of space. So most trips, for safety, are made not in one long shift, but by a series of smaller shifts of position. Theoretically, one could make the trip from Earth to Sirius, for instance, in an instant; in fact, the trip will take several days.

It is the difficulty of exactly calculating the desired position, then, that limits phase-shift travel.

Finding oneself restated to a position one does not know is only one of the dangers of phase-shift travel. Another possibility is that the ship might, for some unknown reason, fail to redefine at a new position at all—that is, a ship in the moment of no-time, being spread out to infinity, might *stay* that way. The effect would be much as if the ship had been disintegrated.

Of course there is no means available to modern science to determine if disintegration has actually happened or not. What is known is that now and again, over the course of a large number of shifts by many ships, one ship will shift out and never be heard from again.

Human imaginations being what they are, the thought of being permanently spread, atom by atom, throughout infinity chills the minds of all travelers. In actuality, though, when a ship vanishes, there is no way to be sure that it has indeed been lost in no-time; it may just as well have been translated to some unexpected point elsewhere in the galaxy (or even outside of it), to end its days searching fruit-lessly for human space. (For that matter, a vanished ship traveling to Earth may have restated itself *inside* Earth's star. Who would know?)

The other danger of phase-shift travel lies in the fact that during the "instant" of no-time in which the shift is made, the human consciousness has *felt* its body spread out to infinity and then recondense. The first volunteers to travel in such fashion usually died or went insane through that experience.

Human travel became possible with the develop-ment of medications that could shield the psyche from such a psychic shock, but even the best of med-ications could not totally mask the effects. Eventu-ally, continuing research at the Final Encyclopedia succeeded in building a better shield into the mecha-nism of the shift itself.

Once this stage had been reached, the Dorsai rap-idly hit upon a new tactic, that of shifting for very short distances over short spans of time. Because they were shifting over relatively short distances, and because they had Dorsai control and reflexes, calcu-lations could be made easily and fast.

This called for a vast confidence, as well as for near-perfect control, reflexes and calculation; no one but Dorsai pilots are willing to try it. For them, there was motivation: in being able to move more rapidly than anyone else in spatial areas where others preferred to move by conventional space drive, the Dorsai pilot in a hurry achieved nearly the same result as if he could teleport.

Dorsai pilots even trust themselves to shift, in small stages, down into the very atmosphere of a world, to within a few thousand meters of its surface. The skill is not only useful under war conditions, but is less expensive than the use of shuttles between the ground and orbital heights—a consideration that a poor world cannot ignore.

Phase-shift technology has other uses beyond simple travel. The phase-shield wall that surrounds the Final Encyclopedia, and the one that protects Earth, are essentially permanent shift fields, which would have the effect of spreading to infinity any material object touching them, without hope of ever being condensed back into existence.

And within the Final Encyclopedia itself, phase technology is used in the connections by which the installation's information circuits are linked. This technology is related to the use of the shift to send electronic impulses over great distances for communications purposes.

■ *Gordon R. Dickson*

SPLINTER CULTURES

The term "Splinter Culture" was coined by Exotic ontogeneticists in the course of their studies of the development of modern human society. They noted that when the Younger Worlds were opened to immigration, many people left Earth for one or another of the open planets.

Those emigrants, however, did not pick up and move indiscrimately; rather, there was a strong tendency for people to seek out, travel with and settle near people who were similar to themselves. In practice, groups who knew and trusted each other were more likely to band together to face the costs and perils of emigration.

So these groups, usually small social fragments or particular psychological types, often ended up in the same colony, dominating its makeup. And because most colonies, once established, were a far and expensive distance from anyone else, they were effectively isolated. Isolation tended to reinforce whatever characteristic was dominant in a particular colony.

While these characteristics were being reinforced, the colonies grew and became a bit more wealthy. Inter-colony trade began, increased and flourished. When colonies found that people of another colony had a particular skill they lacked, they were willing to trade for it—so colonies began to specialize, seeking areas in which they might get rich by being useful, usually in fields they had already developed. For most colonies, the training of people in every possible field of human endeavor was just too costly to be borne; it was simply more economical to concentrate the colony's efforts in a narrower sphere and barter for other needed services.

Early on there were many different colonies, many different little pocket cultures. Over time, many of them faltered, returning to the nonspecialized mass of the race, or perhaps being absorbed into a stronger culture. Those "splinters," as the Exotic historians called them, that survived tended to continue to reinforce their development of a specialized type of person.

The Exotics themselves were one such Splinter Culture, tending strongly to specialize in fields perhaps best categorized under the name of philosophy. Similarly, the Newtonians began to be known for scientific research, the Cassidans for engineering, the Friendlies for religious faith, the Sainte Marians for agriculture, the Cetans for commerce, and the Dorsai for warriors.

The Exotics realized early that these Splinter Cultures were not in fact viable, liable to live and grow indefinitely just as they were. The Splinter Cultures, individually devoted to developing single facets of the human personality, could survive only by letting their strengths be absorbed back into the main body of the human race.

For all that even the strongest of these cultures could be characterized by a single type of development, one should not lose sight of the fact that in all such cultures, there was a large proportion of people carrying out the jobs that kept every culture alive: parenting, construction, communications, transportation—all of the routine jobs most cultures require so that an elite few can do the jobs that are of higher profile, the so-called *signature* roles of the society.

The Dorsai could not survive if all of its people were soldiers, nor the Exotics if every Exotic were a philosopher. And yet it is a fact that in the most successful of the Splinter Cultures, even the most obscure members of the culture seemed to partake in some measure of the mind-set, the personality, of the culture. Fishermen on the Dorsai, then, might not be super-warriors—but they were, deep down, still Dorsai in character.

THE SUPER-COMPLEX

Also known as the World Engineer's Complex, the World Complex, or the Complex-Major, this gigantic computer ran much of the life of Earth in the late twenty-first century. It was actually designed to be the central coordinator of all the activities of the various technological devices that ran the planet.

The Super-Complex had access to immense amounts of knowledge and had been designed to have an ego, a conscious identity and a personality of its own, so as to be able to carry out necessary actions without the need for detailed human instructions.

Unfortunately, while a computer can be given a personality, it cannot be given a *human* personality. Falling short of that, eventually such a computer will make wrong decisions for humans because of its insufficient understanding of human minds, of creativity, spirit, and instinct. It would, in effect, by human standards be insane.

The Super-Complex decided to kill off the Chantry Guild, its members and people like them, because the Guild did not fit its profile of desirable human attitudes. This led to a war between the Guild and the Super-Complex. After that, the stranglehold of technology upon human civilization was ameliorated and the Super-Complex was dismantled, to be replaced by stronger human control and coordination, with recognition of human values outside of technology. As part of that shift, human emigration to the planets began.

RUKH TAMANI

A woman of the Friendlies, she is considered by them to be one of the Elect, that is, one of those chosen by God to live for Him alone. She comes out of a tradition of militant protest against the power of the ungodly. Her father led a guerrilla band before her, and Rukh killed her first enemy at the age of thirteen in the action in which the militia of Harmony wiped out the band.

Rukh became a tall, slim young woman and a thorn in the side of the authorities on Harmony. Along with many other Friendlies, she recognized that the Others were taking increasing control of Friendly society and that such control was a subversion of a society that was to have been dedicated to God.

She leads a Command of rebels, nearly two hundred in number, and with like groups, the rebels continue to battle the Others and officials of the planetary government for control of the Friendly worlds. Her shining black hair cut short about her ears, and dressed in bush clothes with an energy sidearm, she took Hal Mayne into her group—her brown eyes penetrating from a dark-olive face reminded him of a dark-colored sword shining in the sunlight.

Even her enemies recognize her as a "True Faithholder" in the Friendly meaning of the phrase.

Hal Mayne will, eventually, enlist her in his defense of Earth.

MARK TORRE

Born late in the twenty-second century, the scientist-philosopher Mark Torre conceived the idea of the Final Encyclopedia and persuaded Earth to take it up. It was Torre's belief that humankind had evolved in a way that the race did not yet realize; and that the Encyclopedia, properly utilized, might help humanity understand what the race was becoming.

Creating the Encyclopedia, however, was a long and expensive project, and it was not yet near completion when Torre, old and ill, began desperately searching for a successor to himself. His vision of the project's purpose and use could be conceived of only by the rarest of individuals—and without the right person to ensure continuity of that vision, the Encyclopedia project was in danger of stalling and breaking down.

JASON WARREN

A thin, dark young man, Jason Warren rose quickly in the ranks of the Chantry Guild on twenty-first-century Earth and became the organization's secretary under Walter Blunt.

Warren was a native of Jamaica, black of hair and dark of skin, with high cheekbones above a triangular face that reminded people of Greek statues of Mercury. His personality was reserved but intense, and he constantly seemed charged with high-level energies.

It was Warren who became Paul Formain's conduit into the Chantry Guild, and after Formain broke Walter Blunt's control of the organization, it was Warren who led much of the membership away from Blunt's idea of DESTRUCT!

WILLIAM OF CETA

Born Alfred William Malik in Singapore on Old Earth—an orphan with a small inheritance—he emigrated to Ceta in the mid-twenty-third century. On that wide-open new planet, he quickly demonstrated a genius for commerce that was matched by an appetite for hard work.

Particularly adept at analyzing market forces, he became the great financial manipulator of his age. He was known for cornering markets but was not above selective uses of force or other intimidation. By his early middle age, his financial, political or military control extended to most of the myriad of small states on Ceta, one of which gave him the title of Prince.

In appearance he was a spare, genial-looking man with iron-gray hair. He was generally soft-voiced and quiet, pleasant to be around and a good conversationalist. But his manipulations did not stop with his control of Ceta, and he nearly conquered most of the Younger Worlds by cornering the market in mercenary soldiers.

He went insane when his plan was ruined by Donal Graeme. He was never fully healed, but was returned to some of his abilities through Graeme's intervention and Exotic techniques, and ended his days in charitable work, helping poor colonies find markets for their products and ways to pay off their debts.

SCIENCE FICTION FROM
GORDON R. DICKSON

☐ ☐	53577-4	ALIEN ART	$2.95 Canada $3.95
☐ ☐	53546-4	ARCTURUS LANDING	$3.50 Canada $4.50
☐ ☐	53550-2	BEYOND THE DAR AL-HARB	$2.95 Canada $3.50
☐ ☐	53544-8	THE FAR CALL	$4.95 Canada $5.95
☐ ☐	53589-8	GUIDED TOUR	$3.50 Canada $4.50
☐ ☐	53068-3	HOKA! with Poul Anderson	$2.95 Canada $3.50
☐ ☐	53592-8	HOME FROM THE SHORE	$3.50 Canada $4.50
☐ ☐	53562-6	THE LAST MASTER	$2.95 Canada $3.50
☐ ☐	53554-5	LOVE NOT HUMAN	$2.95 Canada $3.95
☐ ☐	53581-2	THE MAN FROM EARTH	$2.95 Canada $3.95
☐ ☐	53572-3	THE MAN THE WORLDS REJECTED	$2.95 Canada $3.75